STICKS aND STONeS
MaY BReaK MY BONeS
BUT WORDS...
THaT'S a WHOLe
DIFFeReNT STORY

FOR MY MAM,
ELIZABETH ANN . . .
THE FIRST SPELL BREATHER

OXFORD
UNIVERSITY PRESS

Great Clarendon Street, Oxford OX2 6DP
Oxford University Press is a department of the University of Oxford.
It furthers the University's objective of excellence in research, scholarship,
and education by publishing worldwide. Oxford is a registered trade mark
of Oxford University Press in the UK and in certain other countries

Database right Oxford University Press (maker)

First published 2019

British Library Cataloguing in Publication Data

Data available

ISBN: 978-0-19-277160-5

3 5 7 9 10 8 6 4 2

Printed in Great Britain

Paper used in the production of this book is a natural,
recyclable product made from wood grown in
sustainable forests.The manufacturing process
conforms to the environmental regulations
of the country of origin.

THE
Last Spell
Breather

JULIE PIKE

OXFORD
UNIVERSITY PRESS

THE MUD BOOK

The Spell wouldn't stay on the shelf. It bounced on the floor and rolled under the kitchen table. Rayne sighed and picked it up for the third time, feeling the scroll softly vibrate. 'Stay there,' she muttered, wedging it underneath a pile of scrolls on the shelf. It was always the same with the Spell of Energy, it could never wait to be released.

She turned to a stack of parchments lying on the table. On top, beautifully inked in Mam's golden script, was the Spell of Sleep. She rolled it up, tied it with twine, and tried to stop herself yawning.

Sunlight streamed through the window, brightening the dimly lit kitchen. Its playful beams danced across the copper pans hanging from the ceiling, reminding her she was stuck inside while Tom and the others were in the orchard. The school bell had rung ten minutes ago. Everyone would be outside now, helping with the apple harvest. Rayne's mouth turned up at the corner. Well, maybe not helping. More like hanging upside down and sneaking apples into their pockets.

She struggled to tie a knot around the last scroll. The Spell of Strength felt heavier than the others, and it took both hands to hoist it onto the shelf. 'All done, Mam,' she said, wiping her hands on her apron. 'Can I go down to the orchard now?'

Mam sat at the other end of the table, hunched over a blank parchment. Her long braids draped across her back out of the way. Deep lines of concentration crinkled the corners of her eyes. 'Just a minute, love,' she said, not taking her eyes off the sheet. Her face began to glow with a golden light; a light Rayne knew had nothing to do with the candles on the table. The light glowed outwards, radiating from deep inside. It shone brighter and brighter.

Rayne's heart skipped a beat as bright inky words swept from Mam's forehead and cascaded onto the parchment like a waterfall. They jostled and circled each other, forming themselves into the lines of a Spell. As the ink dried, the words stilled, and their shimmer dissipated.

Mam sat back in her chair, closing the Spell book at her elbow. 'Sorry, the orchard will have to wait. I need your help in the village this afternoon. Market day is always busiest with people wanting Spells breathed over them.'

'Can't I go out? Just for a bit? I haven't seen my friends for weeks.'

Mam shook her head. 'You knew how it would be when you became my apprentice. You've got too much to learn. There's no time for playing games.'

'But we wouldn't be playing. We'd be helping Farmer Wyn with the harvest.'

Mam grinned. 'I'm not sure Wyn sees it that way.' She held out her freshly written parchment. 'Come on. Roll that up and I'll make us a nice cup of tea.'

Rayne took the Spell. Word-magic tingled into her hand and the muscles in her legs twitched. 'What's this one?'

'What does it feel like?'

Rayne shrugged. 'I don't know.' Lightning quick, she rolled the parchment and put it with the others.

'It's the Spell of Speed.' Mam rose from her chair and went to the fire. Using a tea towel, she unhooked a steaming copper kettle. 'Winter will be here soon. The village council want the Spell to help finish ploughing the fields out by the barrier.'

Rayne rubbed her hands to dispel the tingle of word-magic. 'You could've warned me it was a weird one.'

Mam poured hot water into the teapot. 'If you concentrate on your studies, you'll soon get used to the way each Spell feels.'

Rayne sighed and turned back to the sunlit window, wondering what Tom and Jenna and the others were up to without her.

Mam stirred the pot thoughtfully. 'Perhaps it's time you learned to mindwrite a Spell. You'll recognize them faster then.'

Rayne's eyes slid to the Spell book on the table. She bit her lip. 'Shouldn't we wait? I mean, you always said the Great Library was the best place to learn to mindwrite.'

'It is. But you know the place has been abandoned for years. There's no apprentice school now.' Mam lifted two cups from the dresser and poured the tea.

'Maybe it'll re-open soon?' Rayne murmured.

The teapot clunked on the table. 'It won't. The place is crawling with monsters.' Mam's chair creaked as she sat down. 'You can't put it off any longer.'

I can try, thought Rayne.

Mam spooned honey into both cups. 'I've told

you a million times, there's nothing to worry about.'
She patted the chair beside her.

Rayne's mouth went dry.

She perched next to Mam, her eyes fixed on the
book. It was as wide as her hand and covered in a
thick layer of dried mud. She hadn't been this close
to it for years, not since she was a toddler. Not since
Mam had accidentally left it in reach of her curious
fingers.

Mam pushed a cup forwards. 'Drink up, and we'll
make a start.'

Rayne tore her gaze from the mud book. She
didn't feel like drinking tea.

She felt sick.

ᏏᎦ ᏏᏏᏏ

Candlelight flickered as Mam stroked her fingers
across the muddy cover. 'This Spell book is very
precious. It was given to me by a Word Master,
when I was an apprentice at the Great Library.'

Dark shapes under the mud's surface wriggled
towards Mam's fingers. As she lifted the cover
the dark shapes bobbled into horned heads. They
pushed through the dirt.

Rayne clasped her hands together.

Tiny mouths cracked open, revealing sharp white

teeth. They raced towards Mam's fingers and bit into her soft skin.

Rayne scrunched her eyes shut, sure those bites must hurt, even if Mam said she didn't feel them. 'Your fingers are bleeding!'

'Hush now. It's only a scratch.' Mam took a handkerchief from her skirt pocket and dabbed her fingers. The cloth smeared with streaks of brown and red.

Rayne peered under the cover and frowned. 'Mud devils! Why do you let them bite you?'

'You know why. They're tasting my blood. Making sure it's me. And don't call them devils. They don't like it.'

'What are they then?'

'Grotesques.'

That didn't make them sound any better.

'The Grotesques do an important job making sure only you and I can open the book,' explained Mam.

Rayne sat on her hands. 'What happens if someone else touches it?'

'Bad things. That's why I keep it locked in the chest.' Mam turned the pages. 'Now look, each page has a different Spell listed by the letter of the alphabet. Ah, here's one you'll remember. The Spell of Hearing. I breathed it over the blacksmith last week, remember? All that hammering was making him deaf, poor man.'

Rayne peeped over Mam's shoulder. The centre of each page showed the Spell rhyme, written in neat golden handwriting. The sides of the page were a feast of rich rubies, bright emeralds, and deep sapphires. Mesmerized, she leaned closer. The margins were intricately drawn, illuminating different groups of thumbnail-sized people. Some were deep in conversation, others were herding sheep or shopping at market. There was even a drawing of a blacksmith hammering at his forge.

She frowned. What was wrong with their ears? They were too big, sprouting from their heads at odd angles. Some flew out like giant wings. Others had bulbous lumps of flesh dangling over their chests, pulling the sides of their heads, stretching their faces. 'Why are they drawn like that?'

'Never mind those. They're just silly doodles. Drawn by the Word Master who crafted this book.'

'Doodles? But they must've spent hours and hours drawing them.'

'They don't mean anything. Concentrate on the Spell. Read it aloud, and while you're doing that, picture each word in your mind.'

Here we go again, thought Rayne. Whenever

Mam didn't like a question she always changed the subject. Tucking back her hair, she bent over the page and read the rhyme.

ᗡᖇ THE SPELL OF HEARING ᖇᗡ

Whisper, burble, purr
Clang, chirp, whirr
Sound reverberate
Notice, focus, resonate
Attend when it speaks
Listen to its beats

The words made her ears prickle and she rubbed them.

Mam opened a drawer and took out a clean sheet of parchment. 'Hold this in front of you . . . Now, copy the rhyme onto the sheet with your mind.'

'Copy? How?'

'The way I was taught was, you read the Spell in the book, you see the words in your mind, and then you imagine pushing them from your head onto the parchment.' Mam smiled encouragingly. 'Give it a try.'

Doubting she could mindwrite one word, never mind a whole Spell, Rayne closed her eyes and pictured the lines and curved corners of the words. She gave them a shove and winked open an eye. The parchment was blank. Of course it was.

'Keep trying,' said Mam.

Rayne's heart filled with a sad ache. 'I'm sorry, Mam. I don't think I can.'

'You can,' Mam whispered.

Not wanting to let Mam down, she shut her eyes and pushed again. She pushed until her head throbbed. Suddenly a wetness splashed across her hands. Her eyes flew open and she groaned. The parchment looked like she'd sneezed over it. The ink evaporated, leaving it as clean as before.

Rayne gave a deep sigh. 'It's no use. I'll never be as good as you.'

'Nonsense.' Mam chewed her lip. 'Maybe you have to find the Spell yourself before you copy it.' She closed the book, ignoring the Grotesques rippling across the surface.

A hundred pairs of muddy eyes blinked up at Rayne. A spike of fear shot through her. She leaned back in her chair. 'Do I have to? Can't I learn the Spell by heart?'

'Certainly not. There are hundreds of Spells in here. If you don't copy them, how will you know you've spelt them correctly?'

'Does it matter?'

'Of course it matters,' said Mam, her voice rising. 'Why do you think they're called Spells? If a word is misspelled the magic won't work. Copying is the safest way.'

'Why is it the safest way?'

'Don't worry about that now. At apprentice school I was taught to copy, and that's what you must do.' Mam pushed the book closer to Rayne.

Silence throbbed between them.

'Can I wear my gloves?'

Mam shook her head. 'You heard what I said before. The Grotesques must taste your blood, otherwise they won't let you open the book.'

The cover bristled. A hundred dirty horns pushed through the mud expectantly.

Rayne swallowed. She reached forward.

Grotesque horns surged together forming a large spiky mound. It raced towards her shaking fingers. White teeth gleamed as Grotesque mouths gaped open, ready to bite.

'No!' Rayne shoved the book away. 'They won't bite me again.' It slid across the table and shot over the edge. Mam lunged forward and grabbed it. The Grotesques ripped into her hands with teeth and horns, desperate to stop falling. She clutched the book to her chest and gasped. 'Foolish girl! You must *never* drop the book. If it breaks . . . if the Spells break, it's the end of us!'

Rayne jumped up, her chair grating across the floor. 'Can't we go back to the way things were before? I want to go back to school and see my friends.'

A wave of hurt washed over Mam's face. 'We can't go back. I wish we could, but we can't.' She winced as she laid the book on the table and wrapped her bleeding hands in the tea towel. Bright red patches bloomed on the cloth.

Rayne bolted for the back door and burst into the sunshine. A storm of dried leaves swirled around her feet as she sprinted across the lawn. She skidded to a stop beside the garden gate, trembling.

She focused her gaze through the glassy barrier surrounding Penderin, up to the snow-capped mountains on the other side of the valley. Clouds skimmed their peaks, tinged amber in the afternoon sun. They seemed free, floating where they wanted, drifting over the horizon.

Why wouldn't Mam listen? Every time she tried to say she didn't want to be a Spell Breather they ended up arguing. It wasn't fair. Why couldn't she have had a brother or a sister? Someone who could be Mam's apprentice instead of her?

She wiped a sleeve across her wet cheeks and sniffed. It was no good wishing. There was no one else. She was Mam's apprentice and nothing she could do would ever change that.

THE NEEDS
OF THE MANY

Mam wrapped her arm around Rayne. Together they gazed at the mountains, rising up from the pine-green forest on the other side of the barrier.

'I'm sorry about your hands, Mam.'

She felt a kiss on her hair.

'I'm the one who should be sorry, love. Sorry for making you do something you don't want. But I'm sure if you try you'll come to love breathing Spells as much as me. There's no better feeling in the world than helping people you care for.'

Rayne glanced at Mam's hand on her shoulder, still wrapped in its blood-stained tea towel. Her stomach twisted into a hard knot. 'What if I get it wrong? What if I hurt people?'

'You won't. I'll be here to guide you.' Mam squeezed her shoulder. 'From the first day I arrived in Penderin carrying you in my belly, everyone has been kind to us. We must do all we can to help them in return.'

Rayne stared at her boots. She wanted to help, but they didn't need her. Not really. Mam could easily mindwrite hundreds of Spells for everyone. 'Why do I have to learn now? Can't we wait a bit?'

'It's traditional for Spell Breathers to become apprenticed on their twelfth birthday.'

'I know, but—'

Mam sighed. 'Let's not argue again. We have to leave soon, they'll be queuing for their Spells.'

The knot in Rayne's stomach tightened and she tried to think of a way to keep Mam talking. 'What did you mean when you said if the Spells broke it would be the end of us?'

Mam tensed. 'I didn't mean anything.' She unwrapped her arm from Rayne's shoulder and looked at her hands. 'Come on, I'll breathe a healing Spell over these cuts before we go. Will you fetch our cloaks and the satchel?'

Not waiting for an answer, Mam walked back across the grass to the cottage.

☙ ❧

Rayne trudged down the gravel slope into Penderin. Her satchel bulged with scrolls. Mam strode ahead, her red cloak swirling about her, greeting people and asking after their health. She bent to examine a collie, rubbing her smooth hands across its patchwork fur. No one would have guessed that half an hour earlier her hands had been dripping blood.

They turned into a lane of whitewashed cottages, dodging aside as six fat pigs shuffled towards them, snorting clouds of steam. The hog herder tapped his stick against their backs to hurry them across the lane. He raised his cap. 'Good afternoon, Mistress Meleri. Rayne.'

'Good afternoon, Edgar,' said Mam. 'How's your herd?'

'Back on their feed again, thanks to your Spell.' He nodded towards the village square. 'There's quite a gathering at the meeting hall.' He winked at Rayne. 'Come to see our new apprentice breathe Spells, I reckon. Hope you've got enough scrolls in that satchel of yours?'

Adjusting the strap across her shoulder she forced

a smile. 'We're well prepared, thank you.'

Edgar gave a toothless grin. 'Oho. Maybe I'll stop by later, meself?'

The smile dropped from Rayne's face.

Mam whisked her away. 'See you later then.'

They turned left into a narrow alley between two cottages, their boots squelching into a mix of brown leaves and mud.

'You won't make me breathe Spells over anyone, will you?' Rayne whispered. Everyone would be watching her like hawks. She was bound to mess up.

'Not if you don't want to. Just lend me a hand with sorting the scrolls, that'll be enough for your first time.'

First time, thought Rayne. Meaning there would be other times when she would have to breathe Spells.

They emerged into a wide cobbled lane, clustered on both sides with two-storey houses covered in golden thatch. A hand tapped her back and a friendly voice said, 'Watcha.'

She turned to see a grinning boy with messy blond hair. His breeches and tunic were stained, and there was a streak of dirt across his cheek. 'Tom.' She grinned back. 'Aren't you supposed to be in the orchard? Where've you been to get so mucky?'

'Had to finish something first.' He fell in step beside them. 'I'm on my way there now. You coming?'

'Not today, Rayne's helping me dispense Spells this afternoon,' said Mam. She looked down at Tom's boots. 'How's your ankle? Seems like you're walking better on it.'

Tom rubbed his hand through his hair, making it stick up. 'Better, thank you.'

'I'm glad,' said Mam. 'Though why you spent the summer hobbling around on a strained ankle instead of coming to me, I'll never know.'

'Not everything needs a Spell,' said Tom. 'Some things get better on their own.'

'Perhaps, but it would have been the work of a moment to breathe a healing Spell and saved you a lot of discomfort.'

Tom shrugged. 'There's not a Spell written I'd have breathed over me.'

Rayne elbowed him. He was always bragging about being the only one in the village never to have a Spell breathed over him. He'd probably refuse Mam's help if his leg was hanging off. But it wasn't like him to answer her back.

Mam smiled. 'Not all Spells are for healing. I'm sure one day you'll want a Spell breathed over you.' She strode ahead.

A flush crept up Tom's cheeks.

'What's got into you?' asked Rayne. 'Oh . . . you asked your dad if you could join the bridge guard, then?'

Tom's boots scuffed across the cobbles as they followed Mam. 'He said no. Said it was too dangerous. Said they wouldn't have me, not unless I agreed to having the Spell of Protection breathed over me.'

'Sorry, Tom.' She touched his arm, but he pulled away. 'Look, you knew he'd say that. No one's allowed outside the barrier unless they're protected.'

Tom scowled and dug his hand into his pocket. 'It doesn't matter any more.'

'Fibber. You've been itching to join the bridge guard forever!'

He pulled out his hand and stared at something green and spiky lying in his palm. His eyes lit with sudden mischief.

Rayne leaned across to get a closer look. 'What you got there?'

'Nothing.' He whisked his hand away.

'Oh, don't you start keeping secrets as well.'

He shot a warning look at Mam's back and slipped his hand into his pocket. 'Come to the orchard. I'll show you there.'

She'd have given anything to sneak away for the afternoon but she shook her head. 'I have to help Mam. I can't let her down.'

'Suit yourself.' Tom shrugged and began to whistle. She gave him a sideways glance. Something was definitely up with him.

Metal clanged on metal as they caught up with Mam outside the blacksmith's forge. The smithy swung a hammer against his anvil, beating out a red-hot shoe for the pony tethered in the paddock. Steam hissed as he dipped the shoe in a bucket. Catching sight of Mam, he put down his tools and pointed to his ears. Grinning, he gave a thumbs up.

'What's that all about?' muttered Tom.

'Mam breathed him the Spell of Hearing last week.'

Tom folded his arms.

'What's wrong with that? He'd have gone deaf otherwise.'

'He didn't need a Spell. He could've stuffed beeswax in his ears to muffle the sound of his hammer.'

Rayne pursed her lips. She'd given up trying to persuade Tom about the usefulness of word-magic years ago.

The village square bustled with people. Market

stalls were closing for the day; their owners busily wheeling leftover sacks of fruit and vegetables into the barn in the hall's undercroft. Emerging one by one, some headed home, some headed for the tavern, and—Rayne's stomach squeezed—some joined the snaking queue outside the meeting hall.

Beside the pond, a brood of hens scratched for grain. They squawked and scattered as Rayne and Tom walked between them. 'So, how's Spell Breathing?' he asked. 'Breathed magic over anyone yet?'

She raised an eyebrow. 'You're not really interested, are you?'

'I'm not, but they are.' He gestured around the square. 'It's all everyone's been talking about since your mam took you out of school last month.'

Rayne hunched her shoulders. 'If you must know, Mam's got me practising on plants in the garden.' Yesterday she'd breathed a pruning Spell over a hydrangea. Half the words had landed on its leaves like they were supposed to, the rest had ended up over the well. She'd spent the next hour fishing out the bucket, so Mam could breathe a mending Spell over it. But she wasn't going to tell Tom. He'd only scoff.

Closer to the hall, Rayne began to recognize people in the queue. Ron and Edge the cutler's apprentices were at the back, laughing and hugging sacks of metal tools. Old Flo was bundled in a floral shawl, bent over her stick, coughing. At the top of the steps, by the double doors, a group of women rocked and shushed crying babies. Mam ran lightly up the steps and waved a greeting. Rayne loitered at the bottom.

Tom shook his head. 'Most of them don't need whatever it is they've come for. Ron and Edge are just lazy, they could sharpen those tools themselves.'

'Mam doesn't judge, she helps everyone.'

'Not me,' said Tom, tapping his pocket. He turned away and disappeared in the crowd.

Rayne plodded up the steps, conscious everyone in the queue was staring at her. For the first time in her life she wished more people felt the same as Tom about Spells.

Inside the hall, voices burbled around the rafters as people queued patiently to see their Spell Breather. Mam took the satchel from Rayne, unbuckled the flap and laid out the scrolls on a trestle table at the back of the hall. When she was ready, she turned to a red-cheeked woman at the head of the queue, bouncing a squalling baby on her hip. She smiled. 'Hello, Gwen, how can I help you today?'

An hour later, Mam handed Rayne a blank parchment. 'That's the last of them. Put it with the others will you, love?'

Rubbing the knot in her stomach, Rayne let out a long sigh, relieved she hadn't had to breathe word-magic in front of anyone.

Old Flo shuffled towards the exit, her walking cane tucked under her arm. Rayne sprang to open the double doors. She looked out; the evening sun had cast crooked shadows on the steps. She offered Old Flo her arm. 'It's getting dark. Shall I help you down?'

'Thank you, dear,' said Flo, her gnarly hand patting Rayne's arm. 'There's no need. Now your mam's breathed away my wretched cough and sore throat, I'm as fit as a 90-year-old fiddle. If it wasn't for your mam I wouldn't be here today. None of us would.'

A glow of pride spread through Rayne. 'Mam tries to help everyone.'

Smelling of lavender and tea leaves, Old Flo leaned closer. 'And keeps us safe from the monsters. I shudder when I think how things would be without her barrier.' Her face clouded. 'I notice you didn't breathe word-magic today. Your lessons are going well, aren't they?' Old Flo gripped her arm. 'Everyone's relying on you. Don't let us down.'

'I . . . I'll try not to.'

Old Flo's crinkled eyes searched Rayne's face. She stepped back and sniffed. 'Time I was getting home. You mind your studies now.' Huddling into her shawl, she descended the steps.

A stocky figure hurried into the square pushing a handcart. Nodding a greeting to Old Flo, he stopped outside the hall and hefted three crates into his arms. 'I'm not too late, am I?'

Mam joined Rayne by the door. 'Of course not, Wyn. I thought you might come by after the harvest.'

Farmer Wyn puffed his way up the steps and into the hall. 'Thank you. I've brought the scraps of today's harvest for fattening up.' He lowered the crates to the floor and pushed them in a line. Each was filled with hard green apples, the size of walnuts. 'I'll get the rest,' he said, jogging back to the door.

'Fattening up?' asked Rayne.

'Ripening is what he means.' Mam's fingers skimmed the scrolls on the table. 'Ah, here's the one we need.' She picked up a scroll and offered it to Rayne. 'Why don't you have a go at breathing this Spell?'

Rayne groaned. 'You said I wouldn't have to.'

'It's only a crate of apples.'

Wyn struggled into the hall carrying a stack of crates and laid them next to the others. 'I'll bring in the last of them.' He dashed back out.

'Go on, love,' said Mam in a coaxing voice. 'I'm feeling light headed after breathing so many Spells today.'

Rayne chewed her lip. 'What's the Spell?'

'The Spell of Ripening. You said you wanted to help with the apple harvest. Well, here's your chance.'

Wyn laid three more crates on the floor and stood back expectantly.

Rayne reached for the scroll, then hesitated. 'It's not a weird one, is it?'

Mam guided her to the crates. 'Your hands may feel a little swollen, that's all.'

Rayne took the scroll and immediately her fingers felt fat and heavy.

Wyn plucked a handful of shrivelled apples from the crate and shook his head. 'There's not enough here to feed the village for a day.'

'They'll soon be fat enough for a fortnight's eating,' said Mam, positioning Rayne in front of the line of crates. 'When you're ready.'

The knot in Rayne's stomach twisted again. She broke the twine and her fat fingers unfurled the parchment.

∽ THE SPELL OF RIPENING ∽

Fatten and grow
Thicken and glow
Luscious and fresh
Ripe tender flesh
Swollen and sweet
Plump juicy treat

She drew in deep lungfuls of air. When they were full she pursed her lips and blew gently over the Spell. Light as a feather, the words rose from the parchment and floated towards the crates. The first line of the rhyme fell on the apples like raindrops. Their flesh began to plump and fatten, tripling in size. Rayne stepped forward, blowing the cloud of words over the second crate and the third.

'Well done, love. Make sure every crate gets a share.'

Apple after apple bloomed and brightened. Rayne smiled.

The words hovered and stilled in mid-air. Too late, she realized her smile had caused breath to spill from her mouth. She didn't have enough left to reach the last crate. Spluttering, she watched the last lines of the rhyme fall uselessly into a crate of already ripened apples.

Wyn fiddled with the apples in his hand and began to take a keen interest in the ceiling rafters.

'Don't worry,' said Mam brightly. 'I have another scroll.'

Shamefaced, Rayne stared at the crate of runty apples. Mam should have breathed the Spell, not her. The fat feeling returned as a new scroll was put into her hands. 'There you go. Now make sure you get all the apples this time.'

Determined to get it over with, Rayne knelt before the crate, filled her lungs and blew the word-magic free. She watched with grim satisfaction as the apples swelled and ripened. Farmer Wyn knelt beside the last crate beaming at his new crop. She spied the tiny apples in his hands. There was no way she was breathing the Spell a third time. She blew harder, coughing as the last of the words rushed towards his hand.

'Rayne. No!'

The Spell's inky letters sank into the apples and Wyn's hands and arms. Rayne's eyes shot wide as the sleeves of his smock bulged and stretched and tore down their seams. He cried out as his arms ballooned to the size of tree trunks.

Mam tutted. 'What have I told you about breathing Spells over someone without their permission?'

Rayne cringed, cheeks burning. 'You said to breathe word-magic over all the apples!' Even to her ears, it sounded a lame excuse. At least Mam would have to agree with her now. Her apprentice was a useless Spell Breather.

HALT! WHO
GOES THERE?

Mam turned on her heel and strode to the trestle table. 'I've got a shrinking Spell. Though I can't guarantee it will cancel out the ripening Spell. Sorry, Wyn, your arms may be bigger than they were before.'

The hall doors burst open and a skinny teenager wearing a black cloak hurried towards Mam. 'I have an urgent message from the Bridge Warden.' He reached Mam's side and they put their heads together.

Rayne peeped at Wyn, stooped over his bulging arms and pumpkin-sized knuckles. 'Are you all right?' she asked.

Wyn tried to stand erect, but the dead weight in

his arms was too heavy and he slumped over.

Rayne winced. 'Sorry.' She turned away, so he wouldn't see her tears.

'Now, don't you go worrying,' panted Wyn, craning his neck to look up. 'Your mam will sort me out.' He tried to smile. 'Truth be told I could do with a bit of extra muscle, those crates don't get any lighter.'

Mam finished her conversation and bundled a handful of Spells into her satchel. 'We're needed at the bridge. The scouting party has returned. We have to let them inside the barrier.' She grasped the last scroll and walked purposefully towards Wyn. 'Now hold still. Let's see if we can get your arms back to their right size.'

ᘓ ᘔ

Wind gusted into Rayne's face and her red cloak billowed behind her. The satchel thumped against her hip as she struggled to keep pace with Mam's long strides.

'They're late,' said Mam, raising her voice over the fizz of the swollen river. 'Their protection Spells will wear out soon, if they haven't already. We have to get them inside quickly.'

The stone towers of the bridge loomed overhead. Fire torches flickered above a group of black-cloaked guards milling about its entrance. Behind them the barrier shimmered, stretching along the opposite riverbank like a glass wall. Squinting through the barrier, Rayne saw a man and woman dressed in black sat on horseback. They twisted in their saddles, casting wary glances behind.

The warden, his longsword buckled around his waist, strode up the path towards Mam. He raised an arm in greeting. Rayne felt her face go red as he stared hawklike down his nose at her, his dark brow raised in question.

Mam put her arm around Rayne. 'It's time she knew about the workings of the barrier.'

The warden pursed his lips, then nodded. 'As you wish.' He pointed towards the scouts across the water. 'They've signalled the all-clear. No monsters followed them home.'

'It's good to see them returned in one piece. I was getting worried.'

'All seems well,' agreed the warden. 'The sooner they know we've seen them, the happier I'll be.'

They started towards the bridge. Rayne followed behind. 'It's true then. They really can't see through the barrier?'

'When they look across the water, all they see is a forest of pine trees, just like the ones behind them,' said Mam.

'How do they know where to find the bridge?'

'I've laid a white stone over there,' said the Warden. 'It marks out the bridge entrance. You can't find the bridge or the village on any map. So only those in the know can find it.'

Shouts of laughter made her look down to the water's edge. Tom and Owen were skimming stones into the river. Jenna and Little Jack danced beside them, munching apples, egging them on. She waved and wondered if she'd be allowed to join them. Mam stepped on the bridge and glanced back. 'Coming to help?'

'Me? What can I do?' said Rayne, trudging after Mam to the centre of the bridge.

'To help them push through we'll need to thin the barrier. I always carry a thinning Spell in the satchel, just in case. See if you can sense it.'

Wiping suddenly damp hands on her skirt, Rayne fiddled with the satchel's buckles. The warden and his guards stood to attention around the pillars and watched her intently. Her heart sank. Even Tom was staring up at her, his arms folded. Rayne felt her face go hot. What if she got it wrong again?

Opening the flap, she stared at the scrolls nestled at the bottom of the satchel. Biting her lip, she put her hand in the bag and brushed her fingers against the top scroll. A yawn brewed at the back of her throat. She knew that one. The Spell of Sleep. She touched another, and a giggle burst from her.

Mam smiled. 'The Spell of Laughter. An excellent remedy for melancholy.'

Rayne wished all the scrolls felt like laughter. She moved her hand away and the happy bubble inside her vanished. She touched a third. Her fingers felt flat and flimsy, the opposite of the ripening Spell. She pulled it out. 'This one?'

Mam ran a finger across the scroll and smiled. 'Yes, the Spell of Thinning. See? That wasn't so bad, was it?' She unfurled the scroll.

Flushed with pleasure, Rayne looked at Tom, but he'd turned his back and was skimming stones again.

Raising on tiptoes she peeped around Mam to read the rhyme.

THE SPELL OF THINNING

Delicate as lace
Narrow and slight
Cobwebby sheer
Gauzy and light
Finer than gossamer
Transparent to sight

Mam blew over the words. They sprang from the sheet, sped across the bridge, and sank into the glassy barrier draped over the far bank. A shimmer rippled down its surface. The pine trees behind the scouts brightened, as if they had been freshly painted green. Bending low over their saddles, the scouts rode forward. As they reached the barrier it stretched over their horses' muzzles. Their heads and bodies broke through the membrane, and they clip-clopped onto the bridge.

Mam rolled the blank parchment and handed it to Rayne. 'Now, find the Spell of Hiding. We must seal the barrier straightaway.'

Rayne nodded and touched the remaining scrolls, trying to decipher the different sensations tingling into her hand. What was hiding supposed to feel like? Confused, she tried again, promising herself next time she rolled the parchments, she'd handwrite labels on them.

'Halt, stranger!'

Rayne's head snapped up. The warden sprinted forwards, his eyes focused on the far bank. Behind him the guards pulled out their swords. She spun round. Just outside the barrier was a bearded man holding a long staff. He wore a brown tunic and leggings, and half his face was covered by a leather hood.

Mam froze. '*No!*'

The scouts urged their horses to a gallop, their hoof beats drumming an alarm as they passed by.

The man lowered his hood, revealing a crop of thick red hair. He stared straight at Rayne and smiled from ear to ear. Why was he looking at her? She'd never seen him before. She'd never seen anyone from outside Penderin before.

'Hand me the Spell. Now!' whispered Mam, a hard edge to her voice.

Rayne's stomach knotted. She touched the scrolls again, but still couldn't make them out. The warden ran by, pulling the sword from his belt and pointing the blade at the stranger. 'Stay where you are!'

The man bowed his head but didn't stop smiling. 'Please. I have been walking for days. I seek shelter from the monster plague.'

'You're not welcome here,' bellowed the warden. 'For all we know, you too may have the plague.'

'Come now. Do I look like a monster?'

'Monsters come in many different guises,' said the warden, keeping his sword high.

The man nodded at Mam. 'If you let me cross, your Spell Breather can check me over.'

The warden glanced over his shoulder at Mam's

stony face, then shrugged. 'Spell Breather? We don't have one here.'

'Apologies. My mistake.' The man bowed again.

Mam gripped Rayne's arm like a vice. 'Give me the Spell.'

Heart pounding, Rayne held the satchel towards her. 'I don't know how to find it! Are you sure it's here?'

Without taking her eyes from the stranger, Mam grabbed the bag and plunged her hand inside. 'It's here. It's just hiding from you.' Her eyes narrowed, and she plucked out a scroll.

The smile wiped from the man's face and he raised his hand. 'Wait! Let us not be hasty. I would talk with you.'

Mam snapped the twine and blasted the words off the parchment. They streaked across the bridge and hurtled into the barrier. As it closed over, shimmering light slapped into the man's chest and he shot backwards.

Rayne winced as he smashed into a bramble thicket and lay there coughing. She turned on Mam, eyes wide. 'Why did you do that? He needs our help!'

'He'll be all right.' Mam's voice shook as she rolled the parchment. 'Watch.'

The man groped for his staff and hauled himself

upright. Still coughing, he limped backwards between the trees.

The warden sheathed his sword and shook his head. 'He must have followed the scouts. He'd never have found Penderin otherwise. I'll have a word with them.'

'Who was he?' asked Rayne, bewildered.

'I don't know,' said Mam. 'But one thing's for sure, he's not coming in here.' She slung the satchel over her shoulder and marched off the bridge, almost barging into Tom, who'd climbed up the riverbank. He raised questioning eyes to Rayne. She shrugged and looked back across the water, but the man had gone.

A chill crept down her spine. Mam had never hurt anyone before.

TRUTH OR LIES?

Rayne stepped off the bridge. Mam stood with the female scout, deep in urgent conversation. 'I tell you, Meleri, we did all the usual checks. I'm sure we weren't followed!'

'Kate, you must have been. It's impossible to find Penderin when it's cloaked,' said Mam.

Kate pulled off her leather riding gloves and shook her head. 'I can't understand it.'

The warden joined them. 'I've given orders to double the watch on the bridge, just in case he comes back.' He turned to Kate. 'We were expecting you yesterday. Why are you late?'

'The birds were circling. We had to lay low for a day.' Stepping closer to Mam and the warden, she continued her report in muffled tones.

Rayne glanced towards the riverbank. Tom was huddled with Jenna, Owen, and Little Jack. Behind them, the setting sun glittered on the water like molten gold. It had been weeks since she'd spent time with them. A few minutes couldn't hurt. She looked back at Mam, scowling over something the scout was saying. She turned on her heel and sprinted down the bank. She'd be back before Mam spotted she was gone.

The river swept under the bridge, fine spray misting over the water. Her boots scrunched on wet shingle and she scooped up a handful of flat pebbles. Jiggling the stones in her palm she walked towards the others.

'You're wrong, Tom,' said Jenna, straggles of loose hair dangling from under her lace cap. 'The Spell Breather was right to send him away. We don't know who he is or where he's from.'

'And now we've lost our chance to find out.' Tom nudged a stone from the mud with his boot. 'Maybe he was telling the truth? Maybe he was looking for shelter?'

'Or maybe there was a band of monsters lurking in the bushes waiting to pounce,' said Owen, flicking a stone into the river. 'Maybe they're still there.'

Eyes wide, Little Jack twisted round and scanned the far bank through the barrier. His smock reached down over his leggings like a dress. Spying Rayne his eyes lit, and he toddled towards her. 'Spell Breather. Make the monsters go away. Pleeeease.' He wrapped his arms about her legs.

She ruffled his curly brown hair. 'Don't worry, if there are any monsters out there, Mam will protect us, like she always does.' Over the top of his head she smiled at his sister.

Jenna prised Little Jack's arms free. 'Rayne's an *apprentice* Spell Breather,' she corrected. 'But just like her Mam, you mustn't beg her for Spells.' She threw Rayne an apologetic look. 'He's too young to realize he can't talk to you the same as he used to.'

'I don't mind.' Rayne's heart sank. Why did things have to be different? She wished they could go back to how it was before.

Owen nodded a friendly greeting. 'What does your mam say about the stranger?'

'Oh, you know what she's like, never tells me anything.' Rayne skimmed a pebble into the water and watched it skip twice. 'But I think she knew who he was.'

'I don't get it,' said Tom, flinging a stone across the water towards the barrier. 'The first person we see from the outside world, and your mam blasts him off the bridge. Why?'

Rayne wished she had an answer.

'Because Tom, she's sworn to protect us and keep us safe,' answered Jenna, hugging Little Jack to her.

'Safe from what exactly? How're we supposed to know if nobody will tell us anything?'

Jenna raised an eyebrow and her top lip lifted at the corner. 'The *monster plague* of course!'

'You ever seen any monsters?'

'What's got into you?' asked Owen 'You know we haven't. That's what the barrier's for, to keep us hidden and them out.'

Tom rubbed his hair into a mess. 'But the barrier doesn't stop us seeing out. If there are monsters, how come we've never seen any? Or any scouts from other villages? No one in fact. Until today.'

Rayne's eyes flashed. 'Mam wouldn't lie! And for your information I overheard one of the scouts say the reason they're late is because they had to hide.'

'Hide from what?' asked Little Jack, his eyes as big as saucers.

'I didn't catch it, something to do with birds.'

Tom snorted. '*Birds?* That doesn't sound very monster-like. And the man on the bridge looked as normal as anyone.'

'My uncle's in the bridge guard,' said Owen. 'After his third pint of ale, he'll tell you stories to make your hair stand on end. People with animal faces, children with their legs and arms glued together.'

Little Jack buried his head in his sister's skirt. She put her arms around him. 'Don't frighten him, Owen.'

'Sorry.' He skimmed his last stone into the river. 'The thing is, Tom, what happened on the bridge doesn't change anything. Rules is rules. No one's allowed in, and—'

'No one's allowed out,' finished Tom.

'The scouts are allowed outside,' said Little Jack. 'As long as they're protected by a Spell.'

Tom folded his arms. 'You don't really need a Spell to go outside.'

'You do too. You need a Spell to protect you from monsters.'

'You're wrong.' Tom darted a look at the warden, then dropped his voice. 'You want to know the truth? I went outside the barrier today. And I've never had a Spell breathed over *me*.'

Rayne pursed her lips to stop herself laughing. Jenna nudged Owen in the ribs, and Little Jack giggled.

'It's *true*,' said Tom. 'I've got proof!'

Rayne cocked an eyebrow. 'Like the time you tried to prove one of Mam's Spells had made the keys to the storage barn disappear?'

'Which mysteriously turned up in a box under your bed,' reminded Jenna.

Rayne counted her fingers. 'Then there was the time you—'

'All right, all right.' Tom rubbed his head again. 'This is different. I really do have proof.' Turning his back to the warden he gestured for them to come closer. Owen, Jenna, and Little Jack huddled together. Rayne rolled her eyes.

'Rayne, you asked me earlier what I had in my pocket?' He searched his pocket and brought out something cupped in his hand. 'See,' he whispered, uncurling his fingers. Lying on his palm was a long, green, spiky pine needle.

Rayne gasped. 'Impossible.'

'What is it?' asked Little Jack, standing on tiptoes.

'A leaf,' whispered Jenna, her eyes fixed on Tom's hand.

Little Jack frowned. 'I've never seen a leaf like that.'

Tom grinned. 'That's because it only grows on trees *outside* the barrier.'

'Perhaps it got stuck on one of the scouts' horses?'

said Jenna.

'Or maybe it blew across the bridge when the barrier was thinned?' Owen picked it up and rolled it delicately between his fingers. A faint sweet aroma tingled their noses. 'It's fresh. Hasn't been off the tree long.'

Remembering Tom's strange behaviour with Mam earlier, Rayne shook her head. 'I don't think he's making it up this time. But *how?*'

Tom leaned closer. 'You know we've always been told the barrier goes deep into the ground?'

She nodded.

'Turns out it only goes down about the height of me.'

'How do you figure that out?' asked Owen.

'Because I checked, didn't I? For the last month I've been digging.' He stowed the pine needle in his pocket. 'I broke through earlier today and spent an hour outside.' He grinned at Little Jack's astonished face. 'That's how I know you don't need a Spell to go outside.' He turned to Rayne and Jenna. 'And that's how I know there aren't any monsters, because I didn't see any.'

'You really been out there?' Owen whistled. 'You're brave.'

'Stupid more like,' said Rayne. 'Not seeing a

monster doesn't prove anything. Mam may not say much, but she's forever going on about how dangerous it is out there.'

'She's wrong. I'm going to slip out tonight and spend a week travelling around. Then I'll come back and tell everyone the truth.'

'You can't do that! Your parents will be worried sick,' said Jenna.

Tom flushed. 'They'll end up thanking me. And then they'll know I've been right all along.'

'But what about all of us?' asked Rayne. 'We can't leave the tunnel open for days. *Anything* could get in.'

'The monsters will come and eat us in our beds,' said Little Jack.

'How many times? There is no plague of monsters!' Tom heaved a sigh. 'If it makes you feel better, meet me tonight. You can watch me leave and then fill in the tunnel after I'm gone.' His eyes lit with mischief. 'Even better. When I'm ready, I'll come home over the bridge. The Spell Breather will have to thin the barrier to let me cross, and then everyone will see I'm right.'

'Crazy is what you are.' Owen gave a shaky laugh. 'But all right, on your head be it.'

Rayne and Jenna exchanged uncertain looks.

'Meet me round the back of the hall at midnight

and I'll take you to the tunnel. If you want to tell after I'm gone it won't make any difference to me.' Tom held out his hand, palm down. 'Deal?'

Owen covered Tom's hand with his own. 'Deal!'

Jenna shrugged and added her hand. 'I'd like to see this tunnel. I'm still not convinced this isn't one of your games.'

Little Jack raised his hand.

'Not you,' said Jenna, pulling it aside. 'You'll be fast asleep by then.'

'That's not fair!' he whined.

'Well if you're awake, fine, you can come.' She winked at Tom. 'But if not, I'll show you the filled-in tunnel tomorrow. Come home now, it's time for tea.' She dragged him away.

'I'd best be off too, I've got chores to do,' said Owen. He stumbled backwards up the riverbank, staring at the barrier like he'd never seen it before. 'See you later.'

Tom looked at Rayne. 'You in?'

She planted her hands on her hips. 'If this is another one of your jokes . . . Why did you do it?'

Tom dug up a long thin pebble. 'I never thought you'd actually become your mam's apprentice. You've never shown any interest, have you? For years I kidded myself you felt the same way as me about word-magic.'

'What d'you mean? Mam's breathed hundreds of Spells over me. I'm all for it.' She lowered her gaze . . . as long as someone else was breathing the Spell.

'When your mam took you out of school, I realized you'd take over from her and nothing would change around here.' He drop-kicked the pebble and watched it fly into the water. 'If I don't leave Penderin I'll end up like my parents. I don't want to live off Spells. I hate that they do.'

From the top of the embankment, Mam's voice rang out over the gush of the river. 'There you are! It's time to go. We've got a lot to do.'

Guiltily, they spun around. Mam gestured for Rayne to hurry, then disappeared.

'I have to go.' She started up the bank.

'Wait.' Tom leapt after her. 'You won't tell about the tunnel, will you?'

'Not until I've seen it with my own eyes.' And maybe not then, thought Rayne. After all, Mam was full of secrets. It couldn't hurt to have a few of her own.

⟡

They skirted the village and cut across the meadow, following a winding track back to the cottage. The sun slipped behind the mountains and a scatter of golden stars pinpricked an indigo sky. Mam marched along the path, her braids bouncing on her back.

Rayne caught her up. A deep frown creased Mam's brow and every few minutes she muttered something under her breath. She'd been acting strangely since the bearded man appeared on the bridge. Why hadn't Mam let him in? Was he a monster? Perhaps Tom was right, perhaps they didn't exist any more.

'Mam, what's outside the barrier? Are there really monsters?'

Mam shot her a look. 'What a question! Of course there are.'

'How come we've never seen any then?'

'Count yourself lucky,' Mam snapped. 'I saw plenty before you were born, before I came to live here.'

'The stranger on the bridge didn't look like a monster.'

'*Him*. He's a monster all right. The worst kind.'

'You know him, don't you?'

Mam set her jaw. 'Never mind him. He's gone now and you're safe inside Penderin's barrier. That's all that matters.'

Rayne jogged a few steps to keep pace. 'What's the hurry, then?' She hoped Mam wasn't rushing them home for another mindwriting lesson with the mud devils.

They reached the garden gate. Instead of lifting the latch, Mam turned to Rayne. 'We're hurrying because . . .' she sighed. 'There's no easy way to say this. I'm sorry love, I must leave you for a while.'

'Where are you going? Back into the village?'

Mam shook her head. 'I'm leaving Penderin. I don't know how long I'll be away. But I promise I'll come home as soon as I can.'

Rayne sagged against the fence, dizzy with panic. A hundred questions crowded her brain. Where was Mam going? What would she do? Who would look after the villagers now? Eventually she squeaked out one. '*Why?*'

'There's something I must do. Something I should have done years ago. You're right about the man on the bridge, I do know him. And now he's found us . . .' Mam hugged Rayne close. '*I have to go.*'

෨ ෩

In a daze, Rayne followed Mam through the back door into the kitchen. She watched her hang the satchel on the back of a chair and walk to the hearth. Lifting a poker, she jabbed it into the glowing embers. Flames smouldered to life and licked long shadows up the walls. Despite the warmth, Mam huddled into her cloak.

'Where will you go?' Rayne choked. 'To find the man on the bridge?'

Mam's mouth twisted into a sneer. 'No. But I suspect he won't be far away.'

'Where then?'

'The Great Library.'

'The *library?* You said it was crawling with monsters!'

Mam stowed the poker and strode to the shelf filled with scrolls. 'Which is why I'll be taking some of these.' Her fingers flew across the Spells, pausing every now and then to slide out a scroll and tuck it into her belt.

'What are they for?' asked Rayne, doubting they were healing Spells.

'I'm not sure until I get there.'

Getting answers out of Mam was like trying to get blood out of stone. She had that stubborn look about her eyes Rayne knew well. Her legs wobbled and she sank into a chair, dropping her head in her hands. What would she do without Mam? What about the villagers? They were already treating her differently. It would be a million times worse now. She lifted her head. 'Can I come with you?'

Mam's hand froze. 'No. You must stay inside the barrier, where it's safe.' She turned around. 'And while I'm away, everyone will be relying on you to be their Spell Breather.'

Rayne cringed. 'But Mam, how can I? I can't mindwrite any Spells. And you saw today, I'm *useless* at Spell Breathing. What if I hurt someone?'

Mam crossed the floor in two quick strides and knelt beside her. 'You're not useless. You made a mistake is all. You'll do fine.' She kissed Rayne's hair.

Rayne pulled away.

'And you won't have to mindwrite any new Spells,' continued Mam. 'The shelf is full of scrolls. Plenty enough to help everyone while I'm away.'

Rayne looked at the long wooden shelf running the length of the kitchen, stacked with over a hundred scrolls. How would she ever know which Spells to choose? She held onto Mam's arm. 'Please don't go. The villagers need *you*, not me.'

'I won't be gone long. The warden's explaining everything to the council now. I'll look in on them before I leave and make sure they only ask you for urgent Spells.'

Mam stood up. 'Now, while I'm gone, promise me you won't thin the barrier for anyone to cross in or out. Anyone at all.' She took a quick breath. 'Even me. Do you understand? I'll do that myself when I return.'

Rayne frowned. 'What if you're attacked and need us to come get you?'

Mam went back to the shelf and picked out another scroll. 'Don't worry about me. I'll have this.'

Rayne followed, and Mam gave her the scroll. The muscles in her legs twitched like they had earlier. 'The Spell of Speed?' said Rayne. 'How will that keep you safe?'

'Once I'm outside the barrier, I'll breathe it over myself. I'll be faster than a galloping horse and nothing will catch me. By the time it wears off I'll be at the Great Library.'

'What about the library's monsters?'

Mam forced a smile. 'Stop worrying. I've got a couple of protection Spells for when I get there.' She tucked the Spell into her belt with the others. 'Now promise me,' her voice sounded urgent. 'You won't breathe over the barrier while I'm away.'

'Of course, I promise,' Rayne said, not wanting to breathe any Spells if she could help it. She wracked her brain for a way to make Mam stay. An image of Tom's pine needle bloomed in her head. Would Mam stay if she knew there was a hole under the barrier? 'Tom says—'

Mam strode to the back door. 'I haven't got time for what Tom says. He doesn't know what he's talking about.'

Rayne ran after her. 'You talk to me then. Why are you going to the library? Why are you leaving me?'

Mam turned and cupped Rayne's face in her hands. Her eyes glistened with unshed tears. 'Everything I do, everything I've ever done, has all been for you. To keep you *safe*.' She searched Rayne's eyes. 'One day I hope you'll understand.'

'You're scaring me, Mam. What's wrong? Tell me!'

'When I come home, I'll tell you everything.' She kissed Rayne's forehead and whispered, 'Always remember, *I love you*. First, last, and everywhere in between.' Her hands dropped, and she strode into the night.

Breath rushed from Rayne in a shocked gasp. 'I love you too,' she croaked. But Mam was too far away to hear.

MUD DEVILS

Rayne sat on the windowsill, her knees tucked under her chin, staring into the moonlit garden. A sad ache filled her chest. She kept hoping to see Mam walk through the gate, saying she'd changed her mind and wasn't leaving after all. After thirty minutes, she swung her legs off the sill and stood up. It was no good hoping, Mam wasn't coming home.

Wandering about the kitchen she found herself standing in front of the shelf of scrolls. With Mam gone, everyone would expect her to find the right Spell for their needs. She brushed her fingers across the ends of the scrolls like she'd seen Mam do hundreds of times. A jumble of sensations vibrated into her hand. Hot, sharp, soft, cold, heavy, thick, floaty, wet. Her legs twitched, toes curled, head tingled, throat tightened, heart pounded. 'Stop!' She snatched her hand away.

Everything stilled, except for the wave of questions crashing about her head. Why had Mam gone? What was so important about the man on the bridge, that she'd travel to the Great Library? A place Mam said was filled with monsters. Why hadn't Mam told her? She'd told the warden. Why not her? Another voice in her head whispered, *it's because deep down she knows you're not up to it . . . you're not good enough to be a Spell Breather.*

Rayne covered her face with her hands. How long before she made another mistake? And what if the Spell to put it right wasn't on the shelf? Her eyes slid to the locked oak chest at her feet. If she needed a new Spell, she'd have to mindwrite one from the mud book. She grimaced, imagining sharp, pointy teeth biting into her fingers.

If she was ever going to learn how to mindwrite, the bites would have to stop. Unhooking the key from the wall, she knelt beside the chest and fumbled it into the lock. It turned it with a click.

The lid creaked open.

The Spell book lay in shadow, wrapped in its red velvet cover. She snatched it up and carried it to the table, thumping it onto the surface.

The book hissed.

She dug into the pocket of her cloak and yanked out a pair of thick woollen gloves. Mam wouldn't let her wear them before, but she wasn't here to stop her now. She pulled them on, fingers flexing to make sure every inch of skin was covered. Satisfied, she peeled back the velvet layers, until the book was exposed.

The Grotesques bristled through the mud. A hundred pairs of dirty eyes blinked up at her. She turned her hands from side to side. 'See my gloves? You can't bite through these, so don't bother.'

Setting her mouth into firm line, she picked up the book and held it at arm's length. Hundreds of sharp teeth gnawed at the wool.

'Stop biting. No one in the village is going to touch this book except me and Mam, so you don't have to test our blood.'

The Grotesques ignored her and continued to bite. Remembering how they'd panicked when she'd pushed the book off the table, she gave it a shake. 'If you don't want to be dropped, no biting. Understand?'

She wasn't really going to drop the book, but the mud devils didn't know.

The mud rippled around her fingers. The Grotesques piled over themselves, forming an eager mound of horns and teeth, chomping every inch of her gloves.

Frowning, she shook the book harder. 'I mean it.' she lied. 'If you bite me, I will drop you on your filthy heads.'

A small tear appeared in the wool. Alarmed, she ran to the hearth and held the book over the hot embers. '*Stop.* Or I'll drop you on the fire.'

A wider hole tore open near her thumb. Eyes wide, she watched the mud devils squeeze inside. Her skin pricked. 'Don't you *dare!*'

Sharp teeth sliced her thumb open.

She screamed as bright red blood soaked into the wool.

Her hands opened, and the book fell on the embers in a shower of sparks.

Panic spiked through her. She snatched at the book, its pages fluttered as it flipped into the air and banged down on the hearthstone. Gold inky letters spilled from the pages onto the tiles.

'No. No. No!' She fell to her knees, grabbing the book to her chest and cried out as more letters scattered across the floor.

How could she get them back in? She reached out, but the letters dissolved. Wild eyed she searched the floor, but the letters had vanished.

Legs shaking, she stood and gingerly lowered the book onto the table. She turned the pages to the hearing Spell, not believing her eyes. The Spells were missing letters!

❧ THE SPE L OF HEAR G ☙

W h sper, b ble, pur
lan , hirp, wh rr
Sound reve be ate
Notic , focus, r sona e
Atten whe t speak
ist n to its be

The deformed creatures in the Spells' margins with their bulging ears and stretched skin looked like they were screaming. Rayne groaned. She'd messed up again. Mam would be livid when she came home.

Gently, she closed the cover.

Her swollen thumb throbbed as blood drenched her glove and seeped into the mud. She stared at the blood-stained cover. Jagged cracks had burned deep into the dirt. Each one showed a labyrinth of tiny tunnels. She squinted into one of them ... right into a pair of glaring eyes.

A Grotesque emerged from the tunnel and grew to the size of her finger. Everything about it looked sharp. A dirty horn poked from its head. Long pointy ears, too big for its face, stuck out each side. Two fanged teeth hung over its bottom lip, even its fleshy nose had a sharp tip.

'You burned uss,' it said, lisping through its teeth. 'You bit me!'

Rayne took a steadying breath. Now wasn't the time for arguing. 'I'm sorry. Please, can you help me find the missing letters?'

The Grotesque cackled. 'You won't ssee them again. They've gone. Poof. Vanisshed.'

A dread feeling sank into Rayne's chest. She leaned closer. 'You *must* tell me how to fix the book before Mam comes home.'

The Grotesque laughed so hard it tumbled into the crack. A second Grotesque with bushy eyebrows and a stubby nose crawled up onto the mud and grew bigger. 'Hold your horssess, misssy. We don't have to musst anything. You assk your mother.'

'She says it's your job to protect the Spell book.'

The Grotesque sniffed. 'Tell you that, did sshe? Sshe'd lie through her teeth, that one.'

'What do you mean? Mam doesn't lie.'

Still snickering, the first Grotesque emerged from the mud. 'You've done it now. All your Sspells are broken. Only a Word Masster can resstore letterss to their rightful Sspellss.'

The Grotesque with bushy eyebrows chortled. 'And *they* don't exisst no more.'

'Oh yess. It'ss the end of your lot . . . and after what your mother did to uss . . . *good riddance!*'

A wave of panic washed over her. The *end of us*. Mam had said that earlier. But what did it mean?

'Don't wasste your breath, brother.' A third Grotesque emerged from the cover, scratching its horn. 'Sshe'ss not a proper Sspell Breather. If sshe wass, sshe'd know about the warningss in the marginss. And then sshe wouldn't be sstanding talking to uss. Sshe'd be running for it.'

A long, low howl echoed up from the village.

Rayne jumped. 'What's that?'

'Ssounded like a persson crying in *terrible fear*.'

'More like an animal sscreeching in *dreadful pain*.'

The bushy-eyebrowed Grotesque raised his eyebrows in mock fear. 'Whatever it iss, you don't want to find out.'

The Grotesques threw their fat arms around each other and wept muddy tears of laughter.

She glared at them. They were just trying to frighten her. It was only a dog howling. She needed to find Mam before she left Penderin. It didn't matter if she was angry. Only she could fix the book. And once Mam saw the broken Spells, maybe she'd stay after all. 'Enjoy your joke,' she said. 'I'll find Mam. She'll know what to do.'

The Grotesques laughed harder. 'Good idea! We can't wait to ssee her face when sshe sseess what *you've* done.'

Rayne reached for the book, then hesitated. 'Don't bite me, okay?'

The Grotesques stopped laughing. 'We have no choice,' they snapped. 'Your Mother'ss Sspell compelss uss.'

Bracing herself for a pinch of sharp bites, Rayne picked up the book. The Grotesques raced to her gloves and sank their teeth into the blood-soaked wool. Immediately they unhooked their jaws and shrank into the mud. She blinked. Why hadn't they bitten her? Of course. Her stained gloves tasted of her blood. Vowing to always wear her gloves, she wrapped the book back in its red velvet cloth. Hoisting the satchel from the back of the chair, she pushed the book inside, squashing the scrolls at the bottom.

She ran to the back door, yanked it open and sped into the night, running full pelt across the grass. She had to reach Mam before she left the meeting hall and headed to the barrier.

She tore open the gate.

A wild shriek echoed up the track to greet her.

MONSTERS IN
THE DARK

Rayne raced down the gravel slope in the moonlight, stumbling on the uneven track. She clutched the satchel to her chest, trying to stop the book jigging about and losing more letters from its Spells.

Laid out before her, the village looked the same as ever; thatched rooftops glowed amber in the flickering torchlight. She sped between a row of cottages and slowed to a jog. Something was wrong; door after door gaped open. Candlelight illuminated the rooms inside. They were all empty.

A shriek rang out behind her. She spun round. Something small and furry, with a very long tail, slithered across the cobbles and disappeared into the shadows.

She shivered and stepped backwards.

A sharp point jabbed into her back and she let out a cry.

A gravelly voice croaked, 'Watch your step, girl.'

Whirling round, she saw a hunched figure wrapped in a floral shawl pointing a walking stick. She peered closer. 'Flo? Is that you?'

'Of course it's me.' Old Flo lowered the cane and clutched her shawl across her chest. The material bulged around her neck. 'I'm just on my way up to see your mam.'

Old Flo's voice sounded wheezy again. Rayne hoped she wasn't going to ask for a healing Spell. 'Mam's not there,' she said, walking around Flo. 'I have to hurry, I'm taking the Spell book to her.'

'Wait a minute.' Old Flo raised her stick again. 'If your mam's not home then who . . . ?' Her eyes slid to a scrap of red velvet poking out of the satchel. '*You've* got her Spell book? What's it doing out here?' Her eyes widened. 'Oh, Rayne,' she croaked. 'What have you done to us?'

Another scream pierced the darkness. Rayne jumped. 'What's wrong down here?'

'What's wrong?' choked Old Flo. 'I'll show you

what's wrong.'

She whisked off her shawl, revealing a huge fleshy bulge around her neck. The bulge thinned out as her head rose up and up.

Old Flo's neck was longer than her arm. It snaked forwards.

Rayne gasped. 'What's happened to you?'

'Don't you know?' Old Flo's dislocated head bobbed inches from Rayne's face, glaring at her. 'The last Spell your mam gave me . . . *you broke it!*'

'I . . . I didn't.' Rayne backed away, her heart pounding.

The old woman grabbed at her.

Rayne lurched sideways. 'I'll fetch Mam. She'll know what to do.'

'*Get back here!*' Old Flo tottered forwards, unbalanced by her overlong neck.

Rayne sprinted towards the square, clutching the satchel. Windows and doorways sped by as she tried to remember the last Spell Mam had breathed over Old Flo. It had been a Spell to cure a cough and sore throat. But how had the Spell broken and done that to her neck?

Up ahead a red glow from the blacksmith's forge spewed over the cobbles. An image of the hearing Spell's illuminated margins bloomed in her brain.

One of the drawings had shown a blacksmith with deformed ears. It was the last Spell Mam had given to the blacksmith. Was that broken too?

She skidded to a halt. Trying to stop panting, she peered inside.

A tall round figure leaned over the anvil, staring into the smoky fire. Its giant shoulders rocked to and fro. The back of Rayne's neck prickled.

She crept inside. Stuffy heat from the fire wafted over her face. 'Hello?' she whispered.

The blacksmith inched around. His muscly arms hugged a fat bundle of cloth, as large as a boulder. Something heavy was wrapped inside because it made him stoop.

'Where's your mam?' he murmured. 'My Spell is broken. I need her.'

Despite the heat, Rayne shivered. 'Why? Are you . . .' Her throat went dry, and she swallowed. '. . . sick?'

The blacksmith winced. 'Don't shout, girl.' His arms opened, and the bundle fell in thick layers around his feet.

Rayne gaped. The bundle wasn't cloth. It was skin.

Its folds reached up to the blacksmith's neck, pulling tight to the sides of his head, stretching his face. Just like the drawing in the Spell book.

Rayne bumped against the wall.

He staggered towards her, arms flung out, but the weight of skin pulled him back. 'My ears,' he moaned. 'They won't stop growing!'

She groped for the doorway, her brain struggling to understand how his Spell had broken.

'Wait.' The blacksmith knelt and gathered up the fleshy rolls of his ears. 'Where is your mam?'

Rayne backed outside, colliding with Old Flo. Her wizened face zigzagged around Rayne's shoulder. *'There you are.'*

Rayne dodged aside. Slipping on the cobbles, she almost lost her balance.

'No,' shrieked Old Flo. 'Don't drop it again!'

Rayne steadied herself against a wall as the blacksmith emerged, his ears bundled back in his arms.

'Stop her,' cried Old Flo. 'She's got the broken Spell book.'

Wide with horror, the blacksmith's eyes flew to the satchel.

Rayne didn't wait to hear more, she sped towards the square. A chill wind licked her face as the meeting hall loomed ahead. Something small and furry sprang at her leg and she staggered sideways to avoid stepping on it. Squinting down she spied a small dog lying on the cobbles, whining.

She blinked. It was wearing striped pyjamas.

The dog yelped. 'Rayne.'

Sure she'd misheard, she crouched and studied its brown furry cheeks and white snout. The blood drained from her face. The dog was Little Jack.

'What's happened to me?' he whimpered. 'I . . . I can't stand up straight. My hands and feet, they're all scrunched.'

She stared at his spaniel's body. Instead of hands and feet, he had fluffy white paws. A soft velvet tail poked from a tear in his pyjama's bottom. It wagged from side to side.

She stroked her gloved hand along his back. What was the last Spell Mam had given him? Something to do with a lost sense of smell. She scrunched her eyes tight, sure that if she found the Spell in the book it would show tiny drawings of dog people in the margins.

'Oh, Little Jack.' Her voice dropped to a whisper. 'I'm so sorry.'

What had she done to her friends? Tears squeezed under her lashes. She'd only wanted to stop the Grotesques biting. Holding the Spell book over the fire had been a stupid way to go about it.

'Is Jenna okay?' asked Rayne, but she already knew the answer.

Little Jack whimpered. 'I don't know where she is, or Mam and Dad. They were gone when I woke up.'

Mam's voice echoed in her head. *If the Spells break. It's the end of us.* Is this what Mam meant? Everyone twisted into nightmares? More tears slid down her cheeks. With Mam gone, she was supposed to keep the villagers safe. But instead she'd hurt everyone.

Rayne shook herself. Now wasn't the time for tears. There was still time to put it right. 'Don't worry. We'll find Mam. She'll make you better.' She tried to sound positive. 'Can you walk on your hands and feet?'

Little Jack whimpered. 'I think so.'

She looked towards the meeting hall, desperately hoping Mam was still inside. She stood up. Her legs shook like jelly.

'Come on then.' She stumbled across the cobbles to the hall steps. Little Jack scampered at her heels.

As she began to climb, a rough hand grabbed the back of her cloak and lifted her off her feet. 'I've been looking for you,' said a furious voice.

Coughing, she clawed at the clasp around her neck. A tall figure in a black cloak shook her. Her eyes unfocused, and re-focused. His face was . . .

empty; a blank ball of flat, smooth skin. Panic bolted through her. *Where was his face?*

'You little fool. You've brought the plague upon us.'

The man's cloak and shirt hung open. Through its string laces she saw a pair of dark eyebrows and charcoal eyes glaring at her. A nose protruded from his ribs, and below that a red mouth sliced across his stomach. Rayne cried out. It was the warden.

Little Jack barked, 'Let her go!'

Finally, her frantic fingers unclasped her cloak and she dropped to the ground, gasping for air.

Little Jack bit the warden's leg. The warden kicked out and Little Jack skidded across the cobbles, squealing.

The warden's fingers dug into her shoulder like nails. He lifted the satchel's flap and pulled out the velvet covered Spell book. 'This must be locked away, before you damage it beyond repair.'

Rayne clung to the book and pulled back. 'Don't touch it.'

A corner of the cloth peeled away, exposing rippling mud.

The Grotesques hissed.

The warden yanked the book out of Rayne's grasp. It slapped onto his chest. He roared and staggered backwards, dropping it in surprise.

'No!' Rayne dived to her knees and caught it in her gloved hands. She looked up at the warden. The face on his chest was pockmarked with red, bleeding bites. The mud devils had tasted his blood.

'Give the book to me,' growled the warden, towering over Rayne.

The mud devils surged into a huge mound. A single sharp-tipped horn sprouted from the mass.

A giant Grotesque head emerged from the dirt. Its menacing eyes fixed on the warden. *'Not worthy!'* it bellowed, opening its enormous sharp-toothed jaws. It lunged at the warden's arm.

The face in his chest registered shock. 'What the—?'

Rayne snatched the book away. Giant teeth snapped, missing the warden's wrist by inches.

Quick as lightning, she jumped to her feet and ran behind him.

His blind, egg smooth face whipped round and his arm flashed out.

She couldn't let him have the book. Mam needed it. She jabbed her boot into the back of his knee. Catching him off balance, he sprawled forward, chest first onto the cobbles.

Across the square, the blacksmith lumbered out

of the shadows, weighed down by his bundled-up skin. A second later the snaking head of Old Flo bobbed beside him.

Rayne called to Little Jack. 'Quick! Hide! I'll fetch Mam for you.'

Little Jack whined and limped into the darkness.

Darting up the hall steps, she slipped through the doors and slammed them shut, ramming the timber bar across to lock them tight.

Panting, she leaned her forehead on the wood. In her arms, the giant Grotesque face sprawled across the cover. Sick bile rose in her throat. 'You were going to bite his hand off. *Why?*'

'Only you or your mother may touch uss.' The grim face rippled as it split back into a hundred tiny heads. 'Only you are worthy.'

Her knees buckled, and she slumped to the floor. She *wasn't* worthy. She'd brought the monster plague to Penderin. The deformed drawings in the Spell book's margins weren't doodles. The Grotesques were right, they were warnings. Somehow, broken spells meant broken people.

She rolled around to face the hall. '*Please* be here, Mam.'

Branches of candles cast shadowy light on the trestle table and a circle of chairs. Her gaze swept the hall. From the benches stacked along the wall to the raised platform at the back of the room, the place was deserted.

The Grotesques melted into the mud. All except the stubby-nosed devil with bushy eyebrows. 'Can't find your mother?' it chortled. 'Sshame.' It sank into the mud, a toothy grin on its dirty face. 'Poor misssy. You're on your own now.'

LAST CHANCE

Trying to keep calm, Rayne rewrapped the cloth around the book and shuffled it inside the satchel. She peeled off her gloves and stored them in the pocket. The scab on her thumb throbbed. If Mam was here, she'd breathe it better.

She had to find her. There was a chance Mam hadn't gone through the barrier yet. But to find out she'd have to slip past the warden and the others. Remembering the platform at the back of the hall had a trapdoor down to the undercroft, she got to her feet. Passing the circle of chairs, a curtain to her left twitched. A lumpy shape bulged into the coarse brown fabric.

Heart pounding, she walked on tiptoes, her eyes

locked on the growing bulge.

'Pssst,' hissed the shape.

She started running.

'It's me, Tom.' He stepped from behind the curtain, his hair spiked up like wild grass.

She let out a shaky laugh and scanned him from head to toe, checking for signs of plague. He looked the same as ever. Of course, Tom wouldn't be any different. He'd never had a Spell breathed over him.

'What're you doing here?' she asked.

'Eavesdropping on the council meeting,' said Tom, coming to meet her. 'After the stranger on the bridge, I wanted to hear the scouts' report before I went under the barrier.'

Her eyes lit. 'Did you see my Mam?'

He nodded. 'She left with the warden half an hour ago. Said something about leaving Penderin to go to a library?'

Rayne's hopes faded. If Mam had left with the warden, and he was outside the hall, then she'd gone through the barrier already. She sank onto a chair. 'The library is where Mam studied to be a Spell Breather.' She shook her head. 'If only that man hadn't appeared on the bridge, Mam wouldn't have left. And I wouldn't have . . .' her voice trailed off.

'After the meeting finished, everyone left except

the scouts.' Tom raked his hair. '*Something* happened to them. They started screaming. Giant spikes grew out of their faces, their arms, their legs. Sharp, like hedgehog spines.'

Rayne closed her eyes. The last Spell Mam had breathed over the scouts was the Spell of Protection. That must have broken too.

'They ran outside,' he continued. 'I tried to follow, but it's a nightmare out there. Did you see? When I heard someone coming up the steps just now, I hid behind the curtain.'

'I did see. Old Flo, the blacksmith, the warden . . . even Little Jack. They've all turned into . . .' She looked down at the floor and whispered, 'Monsters.'

Tom's mouth dropped open. '*What did you say?*'

'The monster plague, Tom! It's inside Penderin.'

'It's real?' He fell into a chair beside her. 'How did it get in?' His eyes shot wide. 'My tunnel!'

'I don't think it's that,' she mumbled.

Tom groaned. 'I should never have dug it.' He started to pat his face and chest.

She frowned. 'What're you doing?'

'Checking for plague. We've been exposed, haven't we?'

She wished the monster plague had come under the barrier. Wished it *was* Tom's fault, instead of *her* stupid fault. She should tell him. But if she did, he was bound to turn against her.

She had to find Mam, wherever she was. Maybe there was another thinning Spell in the satchel? If she breathed it over the barrier, they could look for her. She opened the flap, then remembered her promise to Mam.

Did it matter now? The plague was already inside Penderin. She let the flap fall. She was already in enough trouble.

A new idea sprang at her. 'Tom. Your tunnel. Can you take me to it?'

'Why? You think filling it in will stop the plague?'

'It's too late for that. We've got to get outside and find Mam. She'll know what to do.' She tried to sound confident, even though Mam could be anywhere between the barrier and the Great Library by now.

'I don't know. I should help my parents. Before I come down with the plague.'

She bit her lip. Tom's parents asked for more Spells than anyone in Penderin. 'If Mam doesn't come home, there'll be no helping anyone.'

The hall door rattled to the beat of angry thumps. 'Rayne!' The warden's voice roared through the timber. 'Let us in. Let us in *now!*'

She shrank back.

Something large and heavy slammed into the door.

They shot out of their chairs.

Another loud crash and the wooden lock cracked down the middle. Its splinters showered the floor.

'One more hit and it'll break,' said Tom. 'We've got to get out of here.'

They raced to the back of the hall and onto the platform. Tom hauled up the trapdoor and they scrambled to find footholds on the ladder below. Crouching down, they pulled the hatch over their heads. As it closed, the hall door burst off its hinges and the warden ran inside. The mouth on his chest bellowed, 'Rayne!'

The trapdoor clicked shut and everything went dark.

୧ଛ ୬ର

The darkness stank of rotten cauliflowers. Rayne and Tom huddled at the bottom of the ladder. Above their heads, rapid footsteps clattered across the floorboards. Every time the feet stilled Rayne cringed, expecting the hatch to fly open and the warden to haul her up. She'd give anything not to look at the face on his chest again.

Tom whispered in her ear. 'It won't be long before they look down here. There's a door at the back, that's how I got in earlier. I'll show you.' He left her side. Something made of glass smashed.

'Stay still!' she hissed.

The footsteps above stopped.

The silence was deafening. She crossed her fingers, hoping the blacksmith with his giant ears couldn't hear them breathing.

The floorboards creaked again.

Tom gripped her elbow. They skirted around a stack of crates and bumped into sacks of grain. As her eyes adjusted to the dark she saw a faint line of brightness to the left.

Something large and furry scuttled across their boots.

Tom tensed. 'I hope that was a rat.'

Heart thumping as her imagination conjured up different possibilities, she launched herself at the bright line. Her fingers grazed an iron latch. She hitched it up and darted outside. Ducking under the paddock fence, she snuck against a post and scanned the empty street. No one was about. It was dead silent.

Tom joined her. Firelight from a nearby torch fell across his face in an amber line. 'If we head around the back of the hall, we'll come to the meadow. The tunnel's not far from there.'

Her heart leapt. 'You'll take me there?'

He nodded. 'If I hadn't let the plague in, they wouldn't be chasing you. I'm sorry.'

Guilt washed over her like she'd been hit by a Spell. She'd tell him the truth soon. Just as soon as he showed her the tunnel.

Tom bobbed under the fence and skittered across the lane. Sliding into the shadows, he beckoned her to follow. She launched herself after him. Halfway across the cobbles a dog barked.

A girl stood in the middle of the lane. Firelight flickered across a hooked beak covering most of her face. Her hands were curled into sharp claws.

'Jenna?' Tom stepped out of the shadow.

'What's happening?' she asked. Her voice sounded nasal, like her nose was being pinched.

Little Jack jumped around her feet. She bent to pick him up. Her talons hooked into his fur and he howled. Dismayed, she let him go. 'Rayne, where's your mam? Little Jack needs her.'

Rayne exchanged a worried look with Tom. 'We're looking for her.'

'She's gone outside,' said Tom.

'Outside the barrier? She found your tunnel?'

Panic flared in Jenna's voice. She held out her claws. 'They're saying it's *the plague!* Oh, Tom. What've you done?'

He hung his head.

'Mam doesn't know about his tunnel,' said Rayne. 'Don't blame him. We don't know the plague came in that way.'

Little Jack barked. 'Why haven't you two changed?'

'We're bound to soon,' said Tom

'That's why we've got to hurry,' said Rayne. 'We're going through the tunnel to find Mam and bring her back.'

There was a stamping of boots on cobblestones. Noise rumbled towards them from the square. 'They're coming.' Rayne snatched a ragged breath. 'Please Jenna, don't tell them you've seen us.'

Little Jack whined.

Jenna glanced behind her. 'Hurry. They're starting to turn on each other.'

Rayne sobbed. 'I won't come back without Mam. Promise.' She grabbed Tom's hand and ran.

The sound of Little Jack's whines grew fainter. Her breath came hard and fast as she raced beside Tom onto the meadow, her hair flying behind.

Angry shouts called out. Rayne looked back.

Torchlight flared beside the paddock. Silhouetted against their glow a group of shadowy villagers loomed over Jenna. She cringed inside. Jenna's arm stretched out, pointing in the opposite direction.

Tom panted. *'Watch out.'*

The ground gave way and Rayne sprawled across the grass. The satchel bumped along the ground. The angry shouts became screams. With a sick sense of dread, Rayne rolled on her back. The villagers were doubled over. Their shadows were changing shape. Some shrank, some grew twice their size.

Tom came beside her. 'What's happening to them? The plague's getting worse.'

The Spells in the book must have shed more letters. She scooped the satchel into her arms and rocked it back and forth. *Everything* was getting worse!

Tom helped her up. 'Can you walk?'

She ignored her throbbing ankle; the villagers were enduring much worse because of her. 'It's fine. We've got to keep going.'

Tom led the way. 'Watch out for more rabbit holes.'

She followed him over a low stone wall into a sheep field, and together they walked up a slope to a patch of ferns sprouting around a group of rocks and boulders. Behind the rocks the barrier glimmered in the moonlight. Through it, Rayne could make out the pine forest and the sweeping foothills of the mountains.

She turned back and looked over the wall. Penderin seemed small enough to fit into her hand. Dots of firelight bobbed across the meadow towards them. 'Tom, they're coming. Where's the tunnel?'

'Don't worry. It's well hidden.' He leapt onto one of the smaller rocks and knelt beside a cascade of ferns draped across two boulders like a pair of curtains. Parting them, he crawled inside.

Hoping he was right, she scrambled onto the rock and crawled between the ferns. As they swished closed, the moonlight winked out. She squeezed into a cramped space beside him, her knees squelching in wet, cabbage-smelling mulch. 'Ugh, what's this we're kneeling on?'

'Dead ferns,' he said. 'Hang on. I'll light a candle.'

There was a sound of metal being struck and a shower of sparks lit the dark. They left bright spots in her eyes long after the sparks faded. Tom swept the candle before them, illuminating a jagged hole, sloping into the hillside. Cold air wafted from the tunnel.

'Earlier today you didn't believe this existed,' said

Tom. 'Are you sure you want to go out?'

Rayne's heart thumped. For as long as she could remember, Mam had warned her about monsters roaming outside. Now they were inside. Only they weren't really monsters. They were her friends. Whatever lay outside, she had to go. Only Mam could save them.

'This afternoon you didn't believe in monsters,' she reminded him. 'Things change. Look, you don't have to come with me. Stay in Penderin, fill in the tunnel and go help your parents.'

He shook his head. 'Like you said, it's too late to stop the plague. I'm going to look for another village. Maybe they'll know a way to help us.' He put the end of the candle in his mouth and crawled into the hole.

Cradling the satchel in her arms, she took a deep breath, and shuffled after him.

OUT IN THE COLD

Rayne groped her way down the tunnel. The air grew colder and the meagre flame from Tom's candle cast dim light on the walls. Worm-like roots poked through the mud, raking her hair. 'How far to the other side?' she called.

'Not far.' Tom's muffled voice echoed back. 'I reckon we're under the barrier now.'

Her hand squished into mud. Imagining sharp teeth gnawing at her fingers, she sped up.

She crawled between planks of wood that were shoring up the tunnel from collapse. How long had Tom spent digging it out? He must have started the minute Mam took her out of school.

The ground sloped up. The darkness turned to

dusty moonlight. It grew brighter as she crawled into a small clearing surrounded by tall pines. Their branches swayed in the breeze. Through the trees, the mountain's icy peak loomed high above, its granite slopes clearer than ever before. Chill air washed over her skin.

'Feels colder out here, doesn't it?' Tom knelt beside a thick clump of long grass, wiping his hands clean.

Wishing she still had her cloak, she took off the satchel and gingerly wiped the dirt from the scab on her thumb.

Something in the trees screeched and flapped over their heads. Rayne jumped. She scanned the tree tops, looking for monsters.

'Just a bird. I heard it earlier,' said Tom. 'I expect there'll be loads of things out here we've never heard or seen before.'

She stood up. 'Let's start looking for Mam. How far are we from the bridge?'

Tom shrugged.

'Don't you know? I thought you spent an hour out here already.'

'I did, but you can't see Penderin from the outside, remember? Look.' He pointed towards the barrier.

She twisted around and gasped. The boulders

were gone, replaced by an image of dense pine trees. She squinted through them, trying to see the thatched rooftops of Penderin. 'It really is invisible. I can't even see the river.'

'Completely vanished,' agreed Tom. 'The bridge is somewhere off to the right. But out here we'd walk past it and never know.'

She hugged herself. What had she been thinking? That they'd come outside, and Mam would be waiting? That there'd be a big sign pointing, MAM THIS WAY? It would take forever to find the warden's white marker stone. Mam would be long gone by then. She hung her head, trying not to think of Jenna's beaked face as she begged for her Spell Breather.

Tom stood abruptly. 'I'm going to look for help. The scouts said there were villages nearby. They've got to be easier to find than a person.' He walked toward the trees.

'Not if they're hidden by a Spell,' said Rayne.

'Oh.' He stopped and rubbed his hair. 'We must do something. And quickly, before we turn into monsters too.'

She took a deep sigh. She couldn't keep it a secret any longer. Mam had kept secrets. Secrets made things worse. It didn't matter if he blamed her. It couldn't be any worse than the blame she was piling on herself. 'Don't worry about the plague, Tom. You're not going to change.'

'How do you know?'

She lifted her chin. 'Because the plague didn't come through the tunnel. It came from a Spell.'

'A *Spell?*' he snorted. 'I don't believe it.'

'Think for a minute. Everyone we met has changed except us. It has to be because of a Spell.'

'But I've never had a Spell breathed over me.'

'*Exactly*. And everyone else has.'

Tom's head jerked back. 'Wait . . . you've had loads of Spells breathed over you. You're the same.' He looked her up and down. 'Aren't you?'

'Of course I am.' She shrugged. 'Maybe being a Spell Breather makes me immune. I don't know. All I know is word-magic caused this because I . . . ' She shuffled, making her swollen ankle throb again. 'It was an accident, okay?'

'An accident?' Tom frowned. '*What did you do?*'

'I dropped Mam's Spell book. The Spells inside broke . . . and somehow that changed everyone. Mam cured Old Flo's sore throat and now her neck is longer than her arm. She cured the blacksmith's deafness and now his ears are dragging on the floor. It's got to be word-magic.'

Tom folded his arms. 'Where did you drop it?'

'On the fire,' Rayne mumbled.

His eyebrows raised.

'I didn't mean to drop it. The book bit me!'

'It bit you?' said Tom, bewildered.

'Never mind.'

His face cleared. 'So this is your fault?'

'Yes.' A flush burned her cheeks. 'I'm sorry I had a go at you about the tunnel. I'm glad you dug it, or we'd be stuck inside now.'

'Why didn't you say before?'

'I thought you wouldn't show me if you knew. You can crow all you like now. It doesn't matter.'

'I don't feel like crowing.' He rubbed the back of his neck. 'Jenna thinks it's my fault.'

'I'm sorry. I'll tell her when we get back . . . if we get back.'

His hand dropped to his side. 'None of this makes sense. How can dropping a book cause all this?'

'I don't know. That's why we have to find Mam. So she can explain it. So she can fix it.'

'Which brings us back to *how?* We've got no clue how to find her, or this library place. And there's no one to ask.'

'Maybe there is.' She knelt beside the satchel and pulled out the velvet bundle. 'This is Mam's Spell book. It came from the Great Library.'

'So?' Tom knelt beside her. 'You think something in here can tell us where to look?'

'Not *in*, but *on*.' She peeled back the velvet cloth.

'Ugh. Why's it covered in mud?' Tom reached out his hand.

She snatched it away. 'Don't touch it.'

The stubby-nosed Grotesque crawled onto the mud. It grew bigger and hissed at Tom.

Open mouthed, Tom sat back on his heels.

'Found your mother yet, misssy?' chortled the Grotesque.

'She's gone to the Great Library. Do you know the way?'

'You think we keep mapss down here?' the Grotesque tutted. 'Sshame you broke your book or you could mindwrite a Sspell,' it snickered. 'Oh, I forgot. You can't can you? Hahahahaha.' It sank into the dirt, laughing so hard it choked on a mouthful of mud.

'What was that?' asked Tom.

'A Grotesque. Mam put loads of them on the book to protect it.'

'Didn't do a very good job, did they? They let you drop the book on the fire.'

For a moment she was tempted to squash his

hand into the mud, so he could feel exactly how the Grotesques protected the book. Instead she wrapped it back in its cover and laid it on the grass.

She should have known better than to ask the Grotesques for help. It wouldn't make any difference if she could mindwrite; the book was broken, and she didn't have any blank parchments. Just some of Mam's scrolls in the bottom of the satchel.

Her face broke into a wide smile. *Mam's scrolls!*

She tipped the satchel and three scrolls bounced onto the ground.

'What're you doing?' asked Tom.

'Looking for a Spell to help us.'

He groaned. 'Stop.' He put his hands over hers. 'They've landed us in enough trouble already.'

'Have you got a better idea?' She jabbed her head towards the barrier. 'We don't know what's going on in there. You heard what Jenna said. They're turning on each other. If they're as angry as the warden, she and Little Jack won't stand a chance.'

Their eyes locked.

Tom stood up and walked away. 'Do it if it makes you feel better. But don't even think about breathing one over me.'

She picked up a scroll. A wave of dizziness swept over her. Leaning into a patch of moonlight, she unfurled the top of the parchment and read the title. The Spell of Sleep. That was odd, the sleep Spell usually made her yawn. She shook her head, it didn't matter, sleep wasn't going to help them find Mam. She tucked it back inside the satchel and the dizziness vanished.

She reached for another scroll. The moonlight seemed to shine brighter, illuminating the forest floor. Unfurling the top of the scroll, she snatched it open.

ᏸᎩ THE SPELL OF FINDING ᏸᎩ

Discern and detect
Discover and direct
Pinpoint compass bearing
Acquire your heading
A guide shall appear
To track, hunt, and steer

A slow smile spread across her face.

The ink fizzed as a handful of golden letters lifted off the page and evaporated. Her smile dropped. Now the Spell looked like the rhymes in the book. Missing letters. *How* was that possible? And more importantly, would it still work?

Some word-magic had to be better than none.

She looked up at Tom, staring into the darkness. Better not tell him the Spell was broken, he'd try to talk her out of it.

'I . . . er . . .' She cleared her throat. 'I've found the Spell of Finding. It could help us find Mam. I'm going to give it a try.'

Tom gave an exasperated sigh. He walked between the trees and leaned against a trunk. 'This is a waste of time,' he muttered, turning away. 'We should look for another village.'

Rayne stared at the scroll. Where should she breathe the words? She wished she knew how to breathe Spells over herself, like Mam. If not over Tom, it would have to be the trees. If there was any word-magic left in the Spell, something would show itself.

She took a deep breath and blew over the words. They sprang from the parchment and swirled into the shadows and swaying branches. She sat back on her heels and waited.

Tom look over his shoulder, then came to stand beside her. 'Let's start walking.'

She glanced up. 'Why?'

'The Spell hasn't worked, and now we've got an audience.' He pointed to a skinny fox, stretched out on a nearby branch. The creature's eyes gleamed in the moonlight. It blinked languidly.

Her shoulders dropped. The Spell was broken after all.

Tom picked up a dead branch and walked towards the fox, poking the leafy end towards its face. 'Shoo.'

The fox yawned. 'Hardly a friendly welcome.' Its voice sounded deep and rich, like a cup of cream and honey.

Tom stumbled and dropped the branch.

Rayne jumped up. 'Who are you?'

The fox raised its eyebrows. 'Come now. I should think that was perfectly obvious. I am your Spell of Finding.'

THE SPELL OF FINDING

Tom shook his head. 'Foxes can't talk.'

'I can,' said the fox. Its white-tipped tail twitched.

Rayne took an uncertain step forward. 'It's one of Mam's spells. Of course it can talk.'

Turning his back on the creature, Tom whispered, 'How do you know? Maybe it's someone with the plague?'

She squashed the blank parchment into his chest. 'I breathed the Spell free. If you'd been looking, you'd have seen me do it.'

She peeped over his shoulder. The fox was watching them intently. Tom was right, though, who'd ever heard of a talking fox? She tilted her head. Something about it looked odd. Its tail and head looked fine, but its body was pancake flat. Its stick legs didn't look strong enough to hold it up. But then, if it didn't look or sound like a normal fox, that must prove there was something magical about it.

The fox raised a questioning eyebrow.

Rayne smiled. 'Hello. My name is Rayne, and this is Tom.'

'Pleased to meet *you*.' The fox inclined its head towards her, ignoring Tom. 'Well now, this is an odd time of night to get acquainted.' It looked towards the image of trees hiding Penderin. 'The lost village. How did you get outside?'

Rayne pointed to the tunnel's entrance. 'That leads underneath the barrier. Tom dug it.'

The fox looked him up and down. 'Did he?'

Tom raised his palms. 'Hang on. Why should we answer its questions? It should be answering ours. How do you know about Penderin?'

The fox gave a withering sigh. 'Did you not hear me? I am the Spell of Finding. It is my job to know.'

Rayne nudged Tom in the ribs. 'Told you.' She turned to the fox. 'What's your name?'

'You can call me Frank.'

'Frank?' scoffed Tom. 'What sort of name is that for a fox?'

Frank's tail swished around its body. 'A

pronounceable one. If you want to know my name in the Vulpine language it is . . .' He tipped back his head and screeched.

Tom winced. Rayne covered her ears.

'Er . . . thank you.' She lowered her hands. 'We'll call you Frank.'

Frank bent his head graciously. 'So then, to business; what is it you wish to find?'

Tom dug into his pockets and hunched his shoulders.

She stepped closer. 'My mother. She's gone to the Great Library. Do you know the way?'

Frank smiled, his black lips parted, baring a string of pearl white teeth. 'Of course. I will be delighted to escort you.'

'Thank you!' Rayne clasped her hands together. Finally she was a step closer to finding Mam.

'Don't be an idiot,' said Tom. 'You can't walk to the Great Library. What about the monsters?'

'She will be perfectly safe with me,' said Frank.

'No, Rayne. You can't trust him.'

'Why not?'

'Because . . .' Tom spread his hands wide. 'He's a fox. Everyone knows they're sly.'

Frank coughed delicately. 'Do not mind me.' His eyes slid over Rayne. 'I can leave you, if that is what you wish?'

She shot Tom a look. 'Don't upset him.' She walked right up to Frank. 'Please. I must find my mother. Her Spell book, I . . .' A flush crept up her neck. 'It broke. And everyone inside Penderin, well, everyone except me and Tom, they've—'

'Turned into monsters,' finished Frank.

'How do you know?'

'My dear, the warnings are as plain as day in the Spell book. Did you not see the monster illuminations next to each Spell?'

She bit her lip.

Tom shook his head 'How come Rayne hasn't got the plague? I've never had a Spell breathed over me, but she's had loads breathed over her.'

'Broken word-magic cannot harm her,' said Frank. 'Her spark keeps her safe.'

Rayne blinked. 'My what?'

Frank raised his eyebrows. 'Dear me, there seem to be a great many things your mother kept secret. Inside you is a tiny spark of pure magic, with the power to make words real.'

She squashed her hand into her stomach. 'Are you sure?'

'Yes or else you could not have breathed the Spell to bring me here. Your mother gave you a part of her spark when you were born, and it has grown inside you ever since.'

She looked down at her boots wishing she'd asked Mam more questions instead of trying to get out of Spell Breathing lessons. Not that Mam would have answered them.

'How far is this Great Library?' asked Tom.

Frank cocked his head to the east. 'Five or six days' walk from here. Fewer if we find a boat to travel upriver.'

'Are there any villages on the way we can ask for help?' continued Tom.

'None.' Frank made as if to jump from the branch. His eyes shot wide and he yelped. Frantically he jerked his head from side to side.

'What's wrong?' asked Rayne.

'My legs. My body. I cannot move them!' His eyes narrowed to amber slits. 'How dare you summon me and make me your prisoner.' Wrenching his head backwards, he tipped sideways and fell off the branch, landing on the ground in a spray of dried pine needles.

Rayne covered her mouth. Apart from his head and tail, Frank's body was nothing but a bag of skin and fur. Gently, she slid her hands under his back and lifted him up. He was as light as her cloak.

Frank craned his head to look at his body and whined.

'I wouldn't do anything to hurt you,' said Rayne.

'You already have. The broken finding Spell you used to bring me here has removed the bones from my body!'

She hung her head. 'I'm sorry.' Here was yet another reason she wasn't good enough to be a Spell Breather.

'*Broken* finding Spell?' Tom looked at Rayne. 'Don't tell me you broke something else.'

'It was broken already.'

'You shouldn't have breathed over it then.'

'I was only trying to make things better.'

'The only way to make things better is to restore the missing letters to the Spell book,' said Frank.

'How do we do that?'

'Inside the Great Library, the Word Masters' Scriptorium has all the tools necessary to mend broken Spells.'

Rayne frowned. 'But the place is abandoned. Who will help us?'

'If your mother has gone there, she will know what to do.'

Hope bubbled inside Rayne. 'What about the villagers? If Mam restores the book, will they be cured of the plague?'

'Of course. Everything will be back to the way things were before.'

'Hmph,' said Tom. 'Until the Spells break again.'

'They won't. The book will be safe with Mam,' said Rayne, firmly. 'I'm going to the library with Frank. You don't have to come with us. This isn't your fault.'

Frank murmured, 'That is debatable.'

'Fine,' said Tom. 'You walk to the library on your own and good luck with the monsters. I'm going to look for another village.'

'A superb idea,' said Frank.

'Look, Tom, I've got no choice. It's the only way to make things right. I have to find Mam. If the Spells she took with her are broken too, she might be in trouble.'

Tom folded his arms. 'Well then, she'll have to rely on herself instead of word-magic.'

Rayne and Tom glared at each other.

Frank's ears twitched. A scrabbling noise echoed from the tunnel's entrance and a deep voice said, 'It slopes up this side.'

A prickle of fear slid down Rayne's spine. 'The warden,' she whispered. 'How did he find us?'

'The scouts must have followed our footprints,'

whispered Tom.

Frank sniffed the air. 'We had better find somewhere safer to argue.'

'Let's leave the fox here,' said Tom.

Frank's tail swished. 'Charming.'

'We're not leaving him! He can't walk because of me.'

The smell of smoke spiked Rayne's nose and a red glow lit the tunnel's mouth.

'Quick, Tom,' she whispered. 'Get the satchel, and Mam's Spell book.'

He nodded and crept towards the tunnel, just as a flaming torch poked above the rim. Flipping the strap of the satchel over his head, he lifted the velvet covered Spell book.

The warden's blind, egg smooth face appeared.

Rayne shrank closer to Frank. He smelled of roses. She draped him across her shoulders and his silky fur warmed her neck.

The warden put the flat of his palms on the ground and crawled out of the tunnel. He twisted the face on his chest left then right, searching the trees. *'Rayne!'*

Careful not to trip over a stone, nor snap a dead branch, Rayne and Tom backed away.

TWO'S COMPANY,
THREE'S A CROWD

Rayne crouched beside a tree trunk. Frank, draped like a furry collar around her shoulders, raised his head and scanned the forest. Tom peered around the other side. 'It must be an hour since we heard the warden crashing about. I think we've lost him.'

Despite the warmth of Frank's fur, Rayne shivered. 'I hope so. I hope he's gone back to Penderin.'

'That is likely,' said Frank. 'It will be harder for him to track our footprints in the forest. And if he continues to search, well . . . he does not know the direction we are heading.'

Rayne yawned, leant her head against the bark and

half closed her eyes. 'Which way are we heading?'

Frank nodded to a yellow glow filtering through the branches. 'East. We should come to the river by midday. Following the river's course we will come to a citadel. The Great Library sits at the very top.'

'Top of what?' asked Tom.

Frank's tail twitched. 'Do you know what a citadel is?'

Tom shrugged.

'Hmph, a shame you pay so little attention to your dictionary studies.'

'Tom prefers doing stuff to learning words,' said Rayne.

'I see.' Frank sniffed. 'A citadel is a fortress, built upon a hill. The Great Library crests its summit. It is a place of learning, a place of wonders.'

'Mam said the Great Library is full of monsters.'

Frank sighed. 'That was true twelve years ago. I cannot say who inhabits it now.'

A twig snapped. Rayne's eyes flew open. A squirrel bounded across the ground and raced up a nearby trunk. She sprang to her feet, scouring the trees for faceless monsters. One might be lurking, and they'd never know until it pounced.

'Let's keep going,' she said. 'The sooner we find Mam and restore the book, the sooner we can go home.'

Tom stood and dusted pine needles from his breeches. 'Where's your home, Frank?'

'A long way back,' he said, softly. His eyes narrowed. 'Will you be leaving us now, Tom? The village of Tregelis lies in the opposite direction. If you are not attacked, you will reach it by nightfall.'

'I thought you said there were no villages?'

'I said there were none on the way to the Great Library.'

'Oh.' Tom dug his hands into his pockets. 'Doesn't matter. I'm staying with Rayne.'

Frank wrinkled his snout and lowered his head on Rayne's shoulder. 'As you wish,' he huffed.

Rayne nudged Tom in the ribs. 'I don't need a babysitter.' She clambered over a fallen trunk and walked through the wood towards the sun, glad he was coming with her.

Tom followed. 'Chances are we'll come to a village. If Frank doesn't keep us away from them.'

'I assure you, I will direct us by the most efficient route to the Great Library.' Frank made a low whine in the back of this throat. 'The sooner we get there, the sooner I get my bones back.'

Guilt washed over Rayne. 'I'm sorry about your bones, Frank.' She ruffled her fingers into the soft fur of his back. 'Can you feel my hand?'

Frank half closed his eyes. 'Perfectly. It is just the spot I would scratch if I could move my paws.'

Tom caught her up and whispered in her ear. 'I know you think he's your magic Spell and you owe him . . . but I don't trust him. We don't know who he is or where he's from.'

Rayne sped up. Tom was wrong about Frank. He had to be, because if he was right, she'd never find Mam.

Frank craned his head over Rayne's shoulder. 'Keep up, Tom,' he purred. 'And keep your eyes peeled for monsters. You never know where one might be hiding.'

ᘛ ᘚ

Rayne trudged up a steep slope. The trees were sparser the further away from Penderin they walked. The sun heated her back, making sweat bead beneath her hair.

Stopping to catch her breath, she turned to gaze across the valley. Penderin's snow-capped mountains were smaller than she'd ever seen them. Somewhere, in the pine forest below, hid the village. She crossed her fingers, hoping everyone would be all right until she brought Mam home.

Frank's snout twitched. 'I smell the river. We may

see it once we crest this ridge.'

'I'll go look.' Tom jogged up the slope.

Taking a last look at the mountains, she turned to follow. With Tom ahead, this was her chance to ask Frank some niggling questions. 'How will restoring the Spell book fix everything? I don't understand how a Spell can break after Mam's breathed over it?'

'It is a long story.' Frank settled his head on her shoulder. 'The simplest answer is to explain that the Spells in your mother's book are not written in normal ink.'

'They're not?'

'Oh no. Those Spells are written in ink siphoned from your mother's blood when she was an apprentice. When you see her mindwrite onto parchment, she is not really mindwriting, she is copying her own Spells. Even after she breathes them free those Spells are merely copies of the originals in the book.'

'Why does she copy?'

'So she can be assured her Spells have no mistakes in them, of course.'

'Mam said copying was the safest way.' Rayne frowned. 'No one in Penderin would believe her now.'

'Do not be so sure. Many years ago, when the first book broke, people learned that if Spells broke, all their copies broke too. But no one worried very much. Isolated incidents of plague were easily fixed by Word Masters. They just filled in the missing words with Spell Breather ink. As a warning they illuminated their margins with the consequences of broken Spells.'

'Sounds daft, copying after they knew the risks,' said Rayne, glad Tom wasn't around to scoff.

'Believe me, copying is a vast improvement over pure mindwriting. That way creates worse problems. Problems that cannot not be easily fixed. Long ago, before Word Masters came along, Spell Breathers would mindwrite pure word-magic, but people rarely sought them out for Spells.'

She liked the sound of that. 'Why not?'

'Back then Spell Breathers did not attend school. Few could spell properly, so their word-magic was impotent and rarely worked. And the Spells that did were fraught with danger.'

Rayne climbed over a boulder. 'Danger?'

'Words can be blunt instruments, my dear. Spell Breathers lacked the vocabulary to nuance their power. For example, breathing the word 'forget' over someone who wants to forget one thing will eradicate their entire memory.'

'How horrible!' She shook her head. 'But monster

plague is worse.'

'I cannot agree. Word Masters' Spells are rapier-like in their precision. They enable us to forget one bad memory, instead of all memories. Copying Spells is much safer. Oh, I grant you, for the last twelve years the plague has been a disaster, but before that Spell Breathers happily copied Spells for hundreds of years.'

Rayne blinked. 'The plague started the year I was born?' A memory stirred. Mam had said she'd seen plenty of monsters before she lived in Penderin. Had she seen the start of the plague? 'What happened?'

Frank sighed. 'That, my dear, is an even longer story.'

The hiss of water reached her ears as she climbed on top of the ridge. Tom was crouched beside a tree. He tapped a finger over his lips and gestured for her to kneel beside him. 'There's someone there,' he mouthed, pointing down the slope to the river.

Rayne crept next to him. Fifty steps below she spied a handful of tattered tents clustered next to a wide stretch of fast-flowing water. The camp was empty apart from a woman holding a pan over a fire. The smell of frying fish wafted up the slope.

'I thought you said there were no people this way,' said Tom.

'I said there were no villages,' corrected Frank. 'Does that look like a village to you?'

'There.' Tom pointed to the back of the encampment. 'Do you see? A boat. Pulled up on the bank, behind the tents.'

Rayne followed the line of his arm and saw a small wooden boat leant on its side with two oars stuck up at an angle.

Frank raised his head from her shoulder. 'Good. If we take the boat now, we may be at the citadel as soon as tomorrow.'

'We can't steal her boat,' said Rayne. 'We must ask her first.'

'Out here, you will learn it is best to take what you want and ask later,' said Frank.

Tom's stomach rumbled. 'The woman looks all right. Let's talk to her.'

'Ask her for some food, you mean?' said Frank.

'Ask her to help us,' said Tom. His stomach rumbled again. 'And if she wants to share her meal, I won't say no.'

Rayne scanned the woman for signs of plague. Bent over the fire, her long red hair hid part of her face, but her arms and body looked fine. The smell of hot butter made her mouth water. 'Perhaps we should ask for help.'

Frank tutted. 'And what if there are monsters in those tents? Let Tom speak to her, while you and I take the boat.'

'They're not really monsters,' said Rayne, thinking about her friends back home. 'They're just people who need help.'

'Different Spells affect people in different ways,' said Frank. 'Some of them do become monsters. That warden of yours, for example.'

Rayne shivered.

They stared at the woman. She turned the fish over and began to hum a lullaby.

'She hasn't got the plague. We'll be fine. Come on.' Tom stood. 'If we're going to row her boat all day, we'll need to eat something.' He walked over the ridge, his boots snapping twigs as he strode down the slope.

Rayne stood up. She couldn't bear it if something happened to Tom as well. 'Come on, Frank. We'd better go with him.'

'This is a bad idea.'

'It will be all right. She's on her own and there's three of us.' She walked over the ridge and crunched down the slope. 'Anyway, she's seen us now.'

The woman looked up, shielding her eyes from the sun. From the pocket of her apron she whisked out a silver tube.

'You'd better keep quiet, Frank. There's no sense letting her know you can talk,' said Tom over his shoulder.

'That is the first sensible thing he has said,' muttered Frank.

Rayne walked into the camp behind Tom, looking the woman over from head to toe. Two booted feet peeped below a long brown skirt. Her hands each had five fingers. And best of all she had two eyes, two ears, a nose and a mouth, right where they were supposed to be.

The woman frowned at them. 'Who are you? What do you want?'

'I'm Tom, and this is Rayne. Please, we need help.'

The woman's eyes crinkled at the edges as she looked them over. Rayne realized with a shock the woman was checking *them* for signs of plague.

'Where are your parents?' The woman scanned the trees on the ridge. 'If they're lying in wait, I'll blow this whistle and my brothers will run up from the river.'

Tom raised his hands. 'No, we're on our own. Please, can we rest by your fire?'

The woman looked up at the treeline one more

time. Slowly, she put the whistle in her pocket and nodded. Tom unhooked the satchel from his shoulder and knelt by the crackling fire. Rayne glanced at the empty stretch of river. 'Where are your brothers?'

'Fishing.' The woman bent to the pan and turned three white slivers of fish. The butter sauce sizzled. 'You two shouldn't be out in the forest alone. It's not safe.'

'Our parents . . . um, they're in trouble.' Rayne crouched next to Tom. 'We're looking for help.'

The woman shrugged. 'Everyone's looking for help.'

Rayne frowned. What did she mean? She glanced at Tom, but he was leaning over the frying pan. His stomach rumbled, loudly.

The woman stood straight and rubbed her back. 'You want some?'

Tom grinned. 'Yes, please.'

'Well, my brothers won't be happy if I give away their lunch. How about a trade? I give you some fish and you give me your fox. It'll make a tasty stew.'

Frank's tail swished.

Rayne sat back on her heels. 'We can't do that, he's our . . .'

'Pet.' Tom patted Frank's head. 'Ever since we found him with his legs broken, he's become our pet. Haven't you, Frankie?'

Frank growled softly. Tom dropped his hand.

'Pity. I haven't had a good stew in a while. What's in your bag?'

'Just an old book.' Rayne pulled it closer.

The woman's eyes narrowed. 'What sort of old book? Show me.' She snatched the satchel. Rayne grabbed the strap and yanked it back. The leather grazed her hands as the woman jerked it left, then right. Tom leaned in and pulled the strap backwards.

'Watch out,' cried Rayne.

The satchel flipped, and the mud book tumbled from its velvet cloth. It bounced on the grass. The Grotesques hissed as the pages splayed open. Inky letters leaked from the Spells and evaporated. For a heartbeat Rayne froze, lost in a nightmare of what might be happening to her friends back home.

'A Spell book,' whispered the woman. She stared at the rhymes, a hungry look in her eyes.

Careful not to touch the mud, Rayne wrapped the velvet cloth back around the cover and hugged it to her chest.

'Where did you get that book?' demanded the woman. 'Who did you steal it from?'

'I didn't steal it. It's my mother's book.'

'Your mother? Liar. There's been no Spell

Breathers around here for years.'

Rayne looked questioningly at Frank. He watched her intently, as if waiting to see what she would do.

The woman took the whistle from her pocket and blew hard. A shrill note pierced the air as she strode to the river. 'Brothers! Brothers, come quickly!' She blew the whistle again.

Tom grabbed the satchel and pulled Rayne to her feet. 'I think it's time we took the boat.'

The woman whirled about. 'Stay where you are!'

Behind her, two scaly faces emerged from the water. Blue gills fluttered under their ears. Wearing only ragged breeches the brothers crawled ashore. As they clambered to their feet, Rayne saw their entire bodies were coated in fish scales.

'Make no sudden movements,' Frank murmured.

Rayne gripped Tom's hand and they inched backwards until the fire was between them and the creatures. 'What are they?' she gasped.

Frank whined, 'Fish-monsters!'

FISH OUT OF WATER

The fish-monsters shuffled forwards, their webbed feet slapping on the mud. The taller one was bald. The shorter brother had long tufts of shaggy hair covering his eyes. He shook his head like a dog, spraying droplets of water. Webbed fingers brushed wet hair from his bulging eyes. 'What is it, sister?' he gargled.

'Look what she's holding.' The woman pointed at Rayne. 'A Spell book.'

The fish-brother shuffled closer. 'Impossible.'

'It's true. I saw its Spell rhymes. Claims it's her mother's, but that must be a lie.'

Rayne heard whispers. Out of the corner of her eye she saw Frank mouthing something into Tom's ear.

'You, girl,' said the fish-brother. 'Where did you find the book?'

Rayne stared at the skin pulled tight across his flat nose, at his grey swollen lips curved down at the corners. Her mouth went dry. 'It's my Mam's,' she croaked.

'You expect us to believe you and your mother are Spell Breathers?'

The bald fish-brother snorted; river snot ran from his nose. He wiped it with the back of his hand. 'I think we'll have that Spell book for ourselves,' he said, nodding to his sister. 'Then we can take these children for a nice swim . . . under the water.'

The woman stalked around the fire. She pushed her long hair over her shoulder revealing blue gills fluttering in her neck. The woman smirked. 'I'll have your fox for my stew after all.'

Rayne half turned, shielding the book with her body. The Grotesques would never let the fish-monsters open it, but she couldn't risk them making the villagers' plague worse.

'Wait!' Tom held up his hand. 'We can *prove* she's a Spell Breather.'

The woman stopped. 'How?'

Tom took out the last scroll from the satchel. 'This is a healing Spell. If Rayne breathes it over all of you it will free you of plague.'

The fish-monsters stared at it, mesmerized.

Rayne saw Frank wink at her and she groaned silently. There was only one scroll in Mam's satchel and it had nothing to do with healing. It was the Spell of Sleep, and just like the others it was probably broken.

Frank's breath warmed her ear as he whispered, 'Breathe the Spell over them and run to the boat.'

Her heart pounded. She didn't want to breathe another broken Spell, not after the last one had taken Frank's bones. But she must do something. If they lost the book the villagers would stay monsters forever. She thought back to Mam on the bridge, breathing the Spell to close the barrier, knocking the stranger over; beginning to understand why Mam had done it.

The tall fish-brother made a sound like a hacking wet cough. She realized he was laughing. 'Get rid of the plague? Never! Half-man, half-fish is better.'

Rayne looked at the scroll. Could she breathe word-magic over three separate people? The apple crates in the meeting hall had been all together and she'd messed that up.

The fish-woman stalked forwards and slid Frank from her shoulders.

Rayne made up her mind. Tucking the book under her arm, she snatched the scroll from Tom. Ignoring its tingle of magic, she unfurled the scroll.

⟢ THE SPELL OF SLEEP ⟣

Placid, drowsy, warm
Relax, snuggle, calm
Flutter eyelids close
Slumber, deep repose
Dance rapid eyes
Wake revitalized

The ink fizzed and she cringed as some of its letters evaporated. The Spell was broken.

'What's the matter with it?' grunted the fish-brother.

'I'll show you,' said Rayne. Gulping a huge breath, enough to fill her lungs all the way down to her boots, she blew the remaining letters at the monsters.

Its first lines plunged into the fish-woman's chest. Her knees buckled, and she collapsed on the grass. Frank flopped from her arms, yelping as he rolled close to the fire.

Rayne almost gasped, but she stopped herself.

She mustn't spill the air from her mouth again.

The remaining words eddied towards the fish-brothers. Worried they would dodge aside, she blew harder, emptying her lungs quicker. A line of words sank into the shaggy-haired monster's shoulder. His bug eyes rolled back. He swayed sideways and crashed to the ground.

The last lines of the rhyme flew over the other brother's shoulder, speeding towards the river. He leered and shuffled forwards.

Frank cried, 'Turn the words.'

Lungs burning, she darted to the left, running around the flying words, breathing them towards the fish-monster. A jumble of letters nicked his scaly arm. The rest shot behind, falling onto the lapping waters of the shore. Rayne gulped in air. There was no more she could do.

Dazed, the bald fish-monster swayed, his blubbery lips hanging open.

Tom punched the air. 'You did it!'

'That may be premature,' warned Frank.

The fish-monster shook himself.

'He is coming around,' said Frank. '*Run.*'

The empty parchment fell from Rayne's hands. Tom scooped up Frank and they raced around the tents towards the boat.

She looked over her shoulder and wished she hadn't. The fish-monster lurched after her, his stretched face twisted in fury. 'Come back!' he bellowed.

Pinning the book to her side, she pumped her arms to make her legs move faster.

Frank's head bounced on Tom's back as he sprinted ahead. 'Look out,' he called.

Clammy webbed fingers wrapped around Rayne's hand, jerking her backwards. 'You're not going anywhere,' he gargled in her ear. She gagged on the sour stench of fish.

'Let go!' She twisted her fingers through his slimy grip and swung her boot back into his shin. He howled and staggered backwards.

She hurried after Tom. He'd reached the boat and was shoving it into the water. The current rolled waves around his legs as he gripped the stern. 'Hurry!' he yelled.

Seconds from him, a hand clamped around her throat. She slipped and fell against the monster's chest. They crashed to the ground. She twisted, cushioning the book against her body, desperate to spill no more letters. The fish-monster tore it from her.

She reached out, but his knee jabbed into her back, thrusting her up and kicking her sideways. She sprawled on the ground, gasping for air.

The monster sat up, and greedily peeled back the velvet layers. 'Mine now!' he gargled, touching the mud cover.

Immediately a mass of tiny heads surged together. The monster howled as the Grotesques tasted his blood. Their heads formed a huge mound. A dirty horn shot up and a giant face emerged, filling the cover. Its menacing eyes fixed on webbed fingers and its jaws snapped open. *'Not worthy!'* it hissed.

Rayne screamed, 'No!' and scrambled forwards.

Crunch. Sharp teeth sliced through the fish-monster's fingers. Blue blood oozed from his fingerless stumps.

She tasted sick in her mouth and swallowed it down.

The fish-monster swayed on his knees, trying to focus stunned eyes on the book.

The Grotesque head split in two and a hundred tiny devils wriggled back into the mud.

Gently, she used the velvet cloth to pluck the book from the fish monster's hands, then watched as he slumped into the shingle.

The stubby-nosed Grotesque crawled out of the mud, spitting silvery scales from its mouth. It looked at the river, then up at Rayne. 'Where are you sstealing uss to now?'

'I'm not stealing you anywhere,' she said. 'We're going to the Great Library.'

Its bushy brows shot up and it dived into the mud. The cover rippled to the sound of eager chatter. Shaking her head, she wrapped the book back in its cloth.

'Are you all right?' called Tom.

She stood, her legs like jelly. 'No.'

He grimaced. 'Those Grotesques are disgusting.'

'Disgusting, but effective,' said Frank. He looked at Rayne. 'I have never before seen a Spell book covered in such creatures.'

Rayne's head snapped up. 'Aren't all Spell books covered in Grotesques?'

'None. Your mother protected her book well.'

'Not well enough,' she said. 'She told me never to drop it. I should have listened to her.' Her voice wavered. 'I should have listened to you, too. We were wrong to come into the camp.'

'No harm done. We are still in one piece.' Frank coughed delicately. 'Not boiling in a pot.'

She stared at the fish-brother, lying at her feet. A spike of fear jabbed at her heart. 'Is he . . . ?'

'No,' said Frank. 'I suspect he has passed out. A combination of shock and whatever word-magic was left in the Spell.'

She looked back at the other fish-brother and sister lying on the grass. 'Are they sleeping?'

'How can they if the Spell was broken?' said Tom, pulling the boat closer to the shore.

'We could look it up in Mam's book, I'm sure the monster drawings in the Spell's margin will tell us.'

'Better to leave,' said Frank. 'They may revive at any moment.'

Rayne pointed to the fish-monster on the ground, blue blood pooling around his webbed hand. 'We have to help him, or he'll bleed to death.'

'Unlikely. Fish re-grow their fins you know,' said Frank, soothingly. 'The best way to help him, to help us all, is to get to the Great Library.'

Rayne sighed. 'You're right.' She waded into the river. Cold water seeped into her boots and sucked at her skirt. She climbed into the boat and Tom handed her the satchel. 'As soon as the Spell book is fixed, we're coming back to check on them,' she said.

'Of course,' murmured Frank.

She clambered over a wooden slat and sat down. Tom hitched his leg and the boat lurched as he hauled himself and Frank on board. 'And then what? You'll magic back his fingers, I suppose?'

The boat rocked and twisted downstream on the current. The breeze lifted Rayne's hair. 'Not me,

Mam will do it.'

'She wouldn't have to do anything if she hadn't stuck those Grotesques on the book,' said Tom.

Rayne looked down at her hands. A cluster of fish scales glistened on her skin. She rubbed them off, but she couldn't rub away the sting from Tom's words. 'You were happy enough to use word-magic to help us escape.'

Tom's cheeks grew red. 'If I could've thought of another way to escape, I wouldn't have listened to Frank.'

'So Spells do have their uses, then?'

Tom hunched his shoulder.

Sighing, she eased the book into the satchel and stowed it under her seat. 'Frank, what did that woman mean when she said there'd been no Spell Breather around here for years? Every village has one, right?'

'Every village I know lies in ruins.'

Rayne gasped.

Tom's eyes narrowed. 'What about Tregelis?'

'The same.'

'But you tried to send me there.'

Frank's ears drooped.

Tom shrugged Frank from his shoulders and handed him to Rayne. She curled him onto her lap.

'I don't understand. If the villages are in ruins, where are all the people?'

'Roaming the country. Some with the plague have formed small communities, like the one you just saw.'

'Where are their Spell Breathers?' asked Rayne. 'Why aren't they protecting everyone, the same as Mam?'

Frank looked away, a sad expression in his eyes.

The boat lurched.

A splash of water showered them, and two webbed hands rose from the river. One clutched Rayne's shoulder and the other fastened around Frank's tail.

She reached for Tom. He sprang forwards.

Her fingers raked down his sleeve.

'Hang on!'

The hand on her shoulder tugged hard. She screamed and jerked backwards, plunging into the freezing, swirling waters of the river.

IN OVER HER HEAD

Ice water sucked air from Rayne's lungs. Clamping her mouth shut, she kicked hard until her head broke the surface. Spluttering, she twisted about, searching the churning water. 'Frank!'

Tom thrust an oar at her. 'Grab hold,' he shouted.

Her wet fingers slipped on the smooth wood. The current swept her away from the boat. She swam towards it, but hardly made headway as her skirt ballooned out, dragging her back.

Tom grabbed the other oar and rowed frantically across the fast-flowing water. When he was close, he leant over the boat's rim and thrust his arms out. 'Take my hands!'

Grasping her hands, he hauled her to the boat's

side. She clutched the rail, coughing.

His hands clamped around her wrists. 'Are you all right? How did you get away from the fish-monster?'

She choked out a mouthful of water. 'It let me go. It still has Frank.'

He tried to pull her in.

'No.' she croaked. 'I have to find Frank. He can't swim without his bones.'

'I know, but if you go under again the fish-monster will catch you.'

She shook her head, wet hair plastered to the sides of her face. 'We can't leave him. We won't find Mam if we do.'

Tom scanned the river, then tried hauling her up. 'Get in. I'm a stronger swimmer than you. I'll go.'

'There's no time.' She wriggled free and took several deep breaths. 'Watch for us?'

Tom set his mouth into a grim line and nodded. 'I'll be right here.'

Gulping one last breath, she pushed away from the boat, twisted her body and dived into the brown water.

Silence pushed against her ears.

Her eyes stung.

Mud particles clouded the water; she could barely see her hands. She swam lower. A tangle of reeds and weeds emerged from the gloom and swayed along the river bed.

The current dragged at her skirt, pulling her downstream. Pointing her hands together, she formed an arrow with her arms and kicked upstream.

Something silver darted close. Adrenalin shot though her, filling her mind with images of webbed hands and bulging dead eyes. She squinted through the gloom. It was only a fish. A real fish.

Curling her knees to her chest, she pointed her arms down to the river floor and swam closer to the reeds. Ice water sucked her energy. Panic drained her numbing muscles. Her kicks became shallower. But she kept on. She couldn't lose Frank.

Her throat gagged. Her lungs burned. She'd have to surface. But if she did, she'd never find Mam, and her friends would be monsters forever.

A shaft of sunlight pierced the water.

There! A dark rust bundle, curled around a knot of weeds.

Frank.

He wasn't moving.

She kicked towards him.

A scaly face loomed out of the dark.

It was the shaggy-haired fish-brother. She darted away.

He didn't follow. He swayed motionless in the current.

Hoping he would stay that way, she swam above Frank and scrunched her fingers into his fur. Lifting him into her arms, she used the last of her energy to kick towards the light.

Her head burst the surface. She twisted on her back and heaved cool air into her hot lungs.

Raising Frank's snout onto her shoulder, she trod water. Her ears drained, and she heard oars splash. Teeth chattering, she tried to swim, but her heavy arms refused to stroke.

Tom called out, 'Hold on, I'm coming!'

Five seconds later he was by her side. She tried to lift Frank, but the water in his fur weighed him down like a sack of stones.

'I've got him.' Tom pulled Frank from her and laid him gently on one of the benches. He turned back, grasped Rayne's arms and heaved her up. She scrambled over the rim and hauled a leg over the side. Rolling her body, she collapsed into the boat, water pouring down her sleeves and out of her boots. She pushed sopping wet hair from her face. 'How is he?'

'Not breathing . . .'

Pulling herself over the bench, she knelt beside them, shivering.

Tom massaged the white fur on Frank's flat chest. 'Come on you bag of fur. Breathe!'

'Wake up, Frank. Please. We need you.' Her face crumpled. 'I wish Mam was here. She'd mindwrite a waking Spell and breathe it over him.'

Frank's eyes blinked open. He turned his head and retched. 'I had rather . . . not receive any more . . . broken Spells . . . thank you,' he coughed.

Tom sat back. 'I thought you'd drowned.'

Frank coughed up river water. 'Still trying to . . . get rid of me?'

Tom raked his hair and grinned. 'Nah. You're not so bad. If you were, you wouldn't be lying there in such a mess, would you?'

Frank shot him a surprised look.

Tom nudged Rayne's shoulder. 'Nice swimming. What happened to the fish-monster?'

She shrugged. 'The Spell must be working again. He's drifting along the bottom.' She squeezed water out of her hair.

'I hope he stays that way,' said Tom, clambering to the oars. He steered the boat into the middle of the current.

Gently, Rayne turned Frank onto his front and stroked water out of his soaking fur. She brushed tears from her eyes. 'I don't know what we'd do if we lost you.'

'No danger of that,' he wheezed. 'No bones broken.'

She smiled weakly. 'Very funny.'

'I felt you pull me up. What you did was very brave and very kind.' Frank swallowed. 'Thank you for coming back for me.'

Rayne smoothed his head. 'You'd do the same for me, if you could.'

Frank's eyes glistened. He turned away.

His head and tail began to quiver. Sure he must be shaking with cold, she lifted him onto her lap and wrapped her arms about him.

Tom pulled a crumpled tarpaulin from under his bench. 'Take this. It will take the chill off you.' He clambered over the bench and wrapped it around Rayne's shoulders.

She pulled it tightly about them.

Tom sat down and lowered the oars. 'I'll row us downstream for a bit, just in case the monster wakes again, then bring us into shore. We'll make a fire and catch our own lunch from the river.'

The tarpaulin stank of dead fish. Rayne wrinkled her nose. She'd had enough fish to last a lifetime.

᠙᠙

Rayne sat beside the river, Frank curled on her lap, snoring. Her legs dangled over the water's edge and the breeze wafted through her woollen socks. Her boots had squelched when she'd jumped ashore, so she'd pulled them off to dry in the sunshine.

A fishing line stretched from her hands and bobbed in the river. On the ground beside her lay five silver carp.

Frank snatched a ragged breath and his eyes shot open. 'Do not take my bones!' Dazed, he stared around until he focused on Rayne. 'Ah. It is you, my dear.'

She cringed. 'I'm sorry about your bones.'

Frank muttered. 'This is not your fault.'

Rayne sighed. 'It is my fault. It's all my fault.'

'Do not be so hard on yourself. It takes years to become a skilled Spell Breather.'

'I don't think I ever will. That's why we have to find Mam. She will make everyone better. I'm only making things worse.'

'Rescuing me from the river was not making things worse.'

'That was different,' said Rayne. 'I'm no good at word-magic.'

Tom clattered a pile of firewood onto the ground. He sank to his knees and pulled thin strips of dead bark from his pocket. Bundling them into a ball, he stacked twigs around it, making a pyramid.

'Let us make a plan for arriving at the Great Library,' said Frank.

'We already have a plan,' said Rayne. 'Find Mam.'

Tom pulled a thin piece of metal and a flint from his pocket. He struck them together. Sparks fell on the twigs and they burst into flames. He looked up. 'After we find her, we mend the Spell book.'

'Right plan. Wrong order,' said Frank. 'We must restore the Spell book first.'

'No. We must find Mam first. We need her to restore the book.'

'The Great Library is vast,' said Frank. 'It was once home to hundreds of people. Within its walls lie many secret rooms and passageways. It could take days to find her.'

Rayne stared at him. Her cherished vision of finding Mam waiting, with open arms, began to fade.

'I can show you how to restore the Spell book,' continued Frank. 'And the sooner we do, the sooner I get back my bones and your friends will be cured.'

Rayne wound in the fishing line, exchanging a frowning glance with Tom. 'Why didn't you say before?'

Frank's ears flattened. 'You asked me only to guide you to the Great Library. But you saved my life, and now I want to do more to help.'

Rayne shook her head. 'Better to find Mam. She will fix the book. We're bound to make things worse if we try.'

'But what if we can't find your mam?' asked Tom.

'Then we'll search out another Spell Breather to help us.'

'We will not,' said Frank.

'Why not?'

'You asked earlier where the Spell Breathers were?' Frank's tail swished, brushing against her legs. 'There are no other Spell Breathers. You and your mother are the last.'

Her heart skipped a beat. 'The last what?'

'The last Spell Breathers. And if we cannot find your mother . . . you, Rayne, *you* will be the last Spell Breather.'

THE LAST SPELL
BREATHER

'The *last* Spell Breather?' It felt like the ground was cracking open and she was plunging down. A memory flashed. Was this why the warden had told the man on the bridge Penderin didn't have a Spell Breather? Did Mam know? Was this another secret she hadn't trusted her with?

Tom stared. 'You mean Penderin is the only village with a Spell Breather?'

'*Was* the only village,' corrected Frank.

Rayne laid Frank on the grass and hugged her knees. She didn't want to be a Spell Breather at all, never mind the last one. 'Maybe they are hiding behind barriers, just like Penderin?'

'All I know is that for many years, as their Spell books broke, and their villages became riddled with plague, Spell Breathers journeyed to the Great Library to restore their books . . .' Frank's ears drooped, 'and no one ever saw them again.'

Fragments of her last conversation with Mam rang in her ears. *Everything I've ever done, has all been for you. To keep you safe.* She dragged on her boots, yanking the laces tight. 'We've got to go. Mam might be in trouble because of me.'

Tom added wood to the fire. 'We must eat first. We need a plan and I can't think on an empty stomach.'

'We haven't got time!'

'Tom is right,' said Frank. 'We had better eat now. We may not have another opportunity.'

Tom skewered a piece of fish and held it over the flames.

Rayne sighed. 'Oh, all right.' She knelt beside him and picked up a stick; smoke pricked her throat. 'Once these are cooked, we're leaving, and we eat on the boat.'

❧ ❧

The boat drifted around a bend in the river. The

further they travelled the wider it became, slowing the pace of the current. Rayne sat beside Tom in the stern. Frank lay curled on her lap, delicately nibbling a piece of fish she held to his mouth.

Tom threw a bone over the side. He rubbed his hands briskly, then wiped them on his breeches. 'So how do we fix the Spell book, exactly?'

'With a Master Book and a bottle of Spell Breather ink,' said Frank.

'Right. And they are . . . ?' asked Tom.

'Back when the Great Library was home to the Spell Breather school, every new apprentice had a sample of their ink siphoned from them on their first day.'

'Sounds painful,' said Tom. 'Where does the ink come from?'

'Mam says it flows through her body like blood.'

Frank nodded. 'I am glad you mother has told you some things. Word Masters used this ink to handscript Spell Breathers' books. Afterwards, when they copied Spells, they were perfect every time.'

'Until their books broke and their letters fell off the page,' said Rayne.

'Spell books are made to be sturdy,' said Frank. 'But even they cannot survive being thrown on the fire. You must tell me some time, the story of how yours came to break.'

A pink stain crept up her cheeks. 'So, we use Mam's ink to fill in the blanks in her Spell book?'

'Precisely. Handwriting the missing letters will restore the Spells and their word-magic.'

'But how do we know what the missing letters are?' asked Tom.

'We refer to the Master Book. A record of all Spells allowed outside the Great Library. But we must be diligent. It is essential the letters are faithfully copied, or else the Spell will remain broken. And once the ink has dried on the page, we cannot change it.'

'We could drop the book again,' suggested Tom.

'Do not think it!' said Frank. 'There would be no way to guarantee which letters fell from the page. We will only get one chance at this.'

A cloud scudded across the sun. Rayne shivered. If they got it wrong, there would be no way to cure her friends. 'I still think we should find Mam first.'

'Your mother carries copied Spells with her. She must know by now her book is broken. If she is in the Great Library, then she too will be looking for the Master Book and her ink. If we enact my plan, the chances are we will find your mother in either the Dictionary Room or the Scriptorium. And if she is in neither of those places, think how much better it will be to find her with a restored book.'

'That's a lot of ifs,' said Tom.

Rayne looked down into the murky water. She wished Mam was here. She'd wrap her in a comforting hug like always and breathe everything better. 'Frank, you're the Spell of Finding. Can't you find Mam?'

'Sadly, my Spell only finds places and lost items, not people.'

'Oh.'

'It is a shame there are no Word Masters left to siphon your ink,' continued Frank. 'They could create for you the Spell of Summoning and your mother would appear before us.'

It wouldn't matter if there were Word Masters to siphon her ink, she wouldn't be able to copy it anyway. Or worse, she'd mess up the Spell and end up summoning Mam's legs or arms.

'There's no harm looking for your mam in the places Frank suggests first,' said Tom. 'There's a good chance we'll find her, or maybe one of those missing Spell Breathers, in the—what did you call it? The Scriptum thingy?'

'Scriptorium,' corrected Frank. 'It is where Word Masters wrote and bound Spell books and it is where Spell Breather ink is stored.' Frank looked up at Rayne. 'Perhaps it is best that you alone restore your mother's Spell book. If Tom writes "thingy" into the book we are all doomed.'

Tom shrugged. 'I've never been interested in Spells. There's not one written I'd have breathed over me.'

'Why?' asked Frank.

'Because there's nothing a Spell can do that we can't do for ourselves.'

'Is that so?' Frank's whiskers twitched. 'What about the Spell of Flying? Or the Spell of Invisibility? You would not care for those?'

Rayne gasped. 'I'm sure Mam doesn't have those in her book.'

'Of course not. Those Spells are far too precious to be allowed out of the library. Your mother's book contains everyday Spells. Only the essentials needed to protect and care for people.'

Tom leaned forward. 'There's really a Spell for flying?'

'Any word can be made into a Spell. If you know how,' said Frank. 'But Spells do not interest *you* of course, Tom.'

He bit his lip. 'Those two would be okay.'

Rayne hid a smile.

'So we are agreed on our plan?' asked Frank. 'When we arrive at the Great Library, we will collect what we need to restore the book first?'

'Looking for Mam along the way,' said Rayne. Lifting Frank from her lap she laid him along the bench. 'It's time we got a move on.' She clambered across to the oars and dipped them in the water. Just because the broken sleep Spell had helped them escape the fish-monsters, it didn't mean Mam's broken Spells would help her. If Mam was in danger she'd never forgive herself.

◦⊱ ⊰◦

They took turns rowing through the afternoon. With every stroke, the mountains grew smaller until they were lost in the distance. When a crimson sun sank below the horizon, Rayne stowed the oars and rubbed her arms. They hurt like toothache. On either side of the river stretched pancake-flat grassland. She missed the gentle hug of the mountains. 'How long before we arrive?'

'Not until morning,' said Frank.

'My turn,' said Tom, clambering over the benches.

She nodded and climbed across to the stern, yawning loudly.

'Try to get some sleep,' said Frank.

'I can't sleep. Not until I know Mam is okay.'

Tom dipped the oars and pulled back. 'Tell me

more about this invisibility Spell. Does it really mean no one can see you?'

Frank huffed. 'Yes, that is the definition of the word invisible.'

A cold breeze rushed up river, rustling the reeds. Rayne picked up the tarpaulin and laid it over her body like a blanket. 'But Tom, you don't need a Spell, not if there's a handy curtain to hide behind.'

'Ha ha.' Tom leaned into his stroke. 'So, will an invisibility Spell let you walk through walls?'

'Of course not. You would need the Spell of Intangibility. Really, Tom, does your school even have a dictionary?'

Rayne shuffled down her seat and looked up at the darkening sky. Towards the east, stardust glistened. Her hand crept over her midriff. She hoped Frank was right about having a magic spark. It was nice to think she carried something from Mam inside her.

The rhythmic dipping and splashing of oars lulled her. She closed her eyes and an image of Mam floated into her mind. In her cupped hands a tiny spark glowed brightly in the darkness.

◌৺   ৺◌

Rayne stretched, her stiff muscles protesting down her back. She rubbed her neck and looked about.

Grey murk surrounded the boat like a cloud. The air was still. They could be anywhere. The only clue they were moving was the sound of lapping water against the hull.

Tom lay slumped over the oars. Frank was stretched out on the bench between them, his large amber eyes blinked up at her.

'Good morning,' he said.

She sat bolt upright. 'Morning? How long have I been asleep?'

'All night. Did you sleep well?'

She shook her head, remembering snatched images of Mam shouting her name. No matter how fast she'd run, she couldn't find her. And chasing behind were Jenna and Little Jack begging to have their Spell Breather brought back to them.

She splashed water over her face, watching the mist turn the colour of honey.

Frank opened his jaws wide and yawned. 'The sun is rising. We will arrive soon.'

She rubbed her chilled hands and blew on them.

'If you carry me again, my dear, my fur will warm you up.'

Rayne nodded and spread his body across her shoulders, grateful for the warmth.

Up ahead a hulking shadow loomed through the

mist; It towered over them, grasping at the sky.

'The citadel,' whispered Frank.

Rayne leant forward and nudged Tom. 'Wake up.'

'Huh?' He rubbed his eyes and yawned.

Before them, a huge sandstone wall rose up from the river, topped with jagged ramparts that looked like giants' teeth. A lane led through an archway, spiralling upwards between a crowded patchwork of whitewashed houses. Tipping her head back, Rayne traced the lane up to a colossal red stone building, sprawled across the summit like a wedding cake. Its glass-domed roof glinted in the sunshine. Above it, tied to a long pole, hung limp a flag.

'That flag once shone like gold,' Frank murmured.

Black birds lifted off the dome, as if spooked by something. They circled the building, cawing loudly.

Tom whistled through his teeth. 'Your mam's in there?'

The sun winked behind the citadel and the boat drifted into its long shadow. Throwing off the tarpaulin, Rayne clambered to the middle of the boat. 'Budge up, Tom.' She picked up the oar closest to her. 'I'll help you row over there.'

Together they pulled against the current, each stroke taking them closer to the citadel, closer to the library, and—Rayne crossed her fingers—closer to Mam.

Ten more strokes brought them alongside steep steps cut into a harbour wall. The boat scraped against stone and juddered to a stop. Careful to keep Frank secured across her shoulders, Rayne scrambled over the side and up the steps. Her legs wobbled on the firm ground.

'Here, take this.' Tom handed her a rope and she tied it to a bollard. She looked up at the wall and the houses beyond.

'It is hard to believe now, but this was once a bustling port and the seat of power for all the lands we have travelled through, and further beyond,' said Frank.

The quay was littered with broken crates and rusting lumps of metal. 'Did everyone flee when the plague came?' asked Rayne.

'Many people fled. Others may be lurking inside.'

Tom jogged up the steps, carrying the satchel across his body. 'Let's steer clear of meeting anyone. I don't care what they're cooking or how normal they look.'

Rayne dodged a clump of thick weeds poking through broken cobblestones and climbed another flight of steps towards the archway. She walked past a tumbledown barn covered in thick ivy.

Tom followed. 'I wonder when the plague started?'

'According to Frank, just before we were born,' said Rayne. She rubbed her fingers along Frank's spine. 'Do you know what started it?'

'Foolishness,' said Frank.

'What does that mean?' asked Tom.

They neared the sandstone arch they'd seen from the river. The interior was made of red stone, carved with thousands of minute, intricate shapes.

Frank's snout twitched. 'Ah, I had forgotten about—'

The arch hissed. The carvings quivered and the red stone began to melt like hot butter. It spiralled anticlockwise, filling the archway until the carvings faced outwards, completely blocking the lane. The wall bristled with thousands of writhing faces; faces with horns and sharp white teeth.

'Oh no.' Rayne stumbled back. 'Grotesques.'

THE GROTESQUERY

Tom backed away from the spinning riot of teeth and horns. 'Grotesques? Like the ones on your book?'

'Exactly. Same faces. Same teeth.' Rayne grimaced. 'What are they doing here?'

'Unfortunately for us, this is where they live,' said Frank. 'The Grotesquery wraps around the whole citadel, guarding it from outsiders.'

'It didn't stop the monster plague coming in,' said Tom

'It could not. The plague started inside,' said Frank.

The writhing mass of clicking teeth swirled faster.

'Walk away,' said Frank. 'The large horned head on your mother's book is nothing to the giant head of the Grotesquery. It can reach out much further than where we are standing.'

She shook her head. 'The Grotesques on the book won't bite me, not like they bit the fish-monster.'

'This is not the same. I assure you, if you give them enough provocation these creatures will bite your head off.'

The crunch of teeth and the fish-monster's oozing fingers filled her memory. But she couldn't walk away, Mam was in the library. She had to get inside. Legs trembling, she edged closer to the hysterical mass of clicks and bites.

The squirming red stone thrashed about at a furious pace. In the centre, Rayne spied a smooth patch. It looked like it had been scraped flat. Around its edges, hundreds of seething eyes popped open and glared at her.

Frank nipped her ear.

'Ow!' Rayne rubbed where his teeth had grazed her skin. 'What d'you do that for?'

'We will receive a much worse bite if we do not step back!'

Out of the corner of her eye something large and angry pushed out of the mass. Heart thumping, she turned to face it. A colossal Grotesque face protruded from the wall. A horn stuck out of its forehead, above two blazing red eyes, a squashed nose and very long, very sharp teeth. The scab on her thumb reminded her she didn't want to get bitten again, and definitely not by a devil with teeth a hundred times larger.

'Leave thiss place,' it hissed.

Frank murmured in Rayne's ear. 'Back away, slowly.'

Her legs itched to run, but she stood her ground. 'Please. Can you help us?'

The giant face cackled. 'The lasst person we helped, hurt uss.' The face thrust forward; hot breath washed over her. 'Why sshould we help you?'

She swallowed against the lump in her throat. 'I'm looking for my mother. I think she's somewhere inside. Maybe you've seen her?'

The Grotesque scowled. 'We do not care. Leave uss, while we sstill let you.' Its massive jaws clicked open and its fangs chomped up and down, almost brushing her cheek.

She staggered back three steps, bumping into Tom. 'What do we do now?'

'We search for another way in,' said Frank. 'There are many secret ways inside the Great Library.'

'How do you know?' asked Tom.

'I would give you three guesses, but we do not have time,' said Frank. 'I am the Spell of Finding, remember?'

They walked backwards. The Grotesque face shrank into the mass of snapping teeth.

'Wait,' said Rayne. 'We have to find out if they've seen Mam.'

The hissing face re-emerged.

She scrunched her hands into fists and stepped forward. 'We're not leaving until you tell us if you've seen my mother. She is a Spell Breather and her name is Meleri.'

The Grotesque's eyes shot wide. Its face twisted, and it let out a furious roar. The stink of dead weeds washed up Rayne's nose. Like a coiled spring, the giant face shot forward, its mouth gaped open, teeth ready to plunge.

Rayne cried out and threw up an arm.

Suddenly, the face whooshed back to the wall and collapsed into the writhing stone. It jumbled and crumbled as thousands of tiny mouths snicked open and closed. It sounded like an angry mob arguing with itself.

Frank's tail swished about. 'It seems the wretched creatures have indeed seen your mother.'

The whirling mass stilled. Slowly, a different face emerged; round and smooth and hornless. Two buck teeth hung over its bottom lip. Hairy eyebrows capped squinty eyes which stared at her. 'Your mother iss Meleri?'

'Yes,' said Rayne, warily.

'Then you are the daughter of the one who sstole from uss!'

Her mouth gaped. 'You're lying. Mam would never steal!'

The head squirmed forward. 'Do not argue with uss or our ssharp-toothed brother will return in our place.' Its eyes raked over her. 'You have the look of our robber. You *are* the daughter of the one who sstole our brotherss.'

'That's crazy. Mam wouldn't steal, just to get inside.'

'Not to get in. To get out . . . twelve yearss ago.'

Rayne frowned.

'You ssee where sshe cut uss? You ssee the sspace where our brotherss once lived? Your mother hacked them from uss, bound them in mud and breathed them onto her book.'

Frank tried to whisper in her ear. She nudged his head away, needing to know more.

'It wass the day the plague began. Your mother wass running away. Sshe leant beneath the arch, ssobbing becausse all the bookss were breaking. Sshe begged uss to protect her book. But we cannot leave the sstone.' The sides of its mouth turned down. 'Sshe took out her knife and ssliced our brotherss away.'

'Oh no!' cried Rayne.

Two red tears welled in the Grotesque's eyes and traced wet lines down its cheeks.

'What happened next?' asked Tom.

'Sshe sstole them from uss. They cried out ass sshe ran away.' Tears splashed onto the cobbles. 'We misss our brotherss.'

Rayne bit her lip. So this was where the devils on the Spell book came from. Mam must have been desperate to do it. She hung her head. 'I'm sorry.'

'We do not want your pity,' it spat. 'We want our brotherss. Where are they?'

Her eyes slid to the satchel strapped around Tom's chest. Mam had put the devils on the book to protect it. She shook her head. It hadn't worked, the book was broken. She slipped the satchel from Tom's shoulder.

'What are you doing?' he whispered.

'Giving them back their brothers.'

'Are you sure? What will your mam say?'

She unbuckled the straps and slipped out the book, wrapped in its velvet cover. 'It doesn't matter. They don't belong on the book. And I can't bear to watch them biting any more fingers off.' She turned to the Grotesquery and lifted the layers of cloth.

'Your brothers are here.'

The Grotesquery spun in a mad frenzy. *'Brotherss!'* The huge face zoomed towards the book and stared at the cover greedily.

The mud cover rippled and a hundred pairs of eyes blinked out of the dirt. One by one the mud devils climbed onto the cover. They stretched out their arms trying to jump free, but they were stuck in the mud.

Hating herself for doing it, Rayne stepped back. 'I will return your brothers. On one condition.'

The enormous face followed her, menacingly.

'Let us pass under the arch, into the citadel.'

Giant eyes lingered on the book, then the face shot backwards and merged into the wall. The red stone clicked and writhed and churned.

Worried the head would spring out and bite the book from her hands, she said, 'Perhaps we should walk back a bit further.'

The noise from the Grotesquery became a deafening roar.

Tom's face drained of colour. 'Good idea.'

They took five steps back.

'More,' said Frank.

'Just how far does that thing come out?' asked Tom.

On the book's cover, the Grotesque with the bushy

eyebrows and stubby nose waved at Rayne. She bent her head to hear what it said. 'You could walk to the river and it would not be far enough, misssy.'

'Frank, I think it's time you told us where the secret way is,' said Tom. 'Fast.'

The roar subsided and the smooth face with buck teeth pushed through the writhing mass. 'Daughter of a thief, we agree to your terms. If you return our brotherss, we will allow you ssafe passsage through the arch.'

'Ask it to promise,' said Tom.

The face glared at him.

Rayne nudged him in the ribs, and they walked slowly to the Grotesquery.

'Any ideas how to take their brothers off the cover, Frank?' Rayne murmured.

'Alas, not.'

Stubby Nose called to her. 'Sscrape the mud off the book. It iss the only way to break your mother'ss Sspell.'

'But they'll bite you,' said Tom. 'You can't drop the book again.'

She tried to sound confident. 'I know. I won't.'

They reached the mass of staring eyes. Kneeling, she gently lowered the book to the ground, making sure the cloth was between it and the cobblestones.

The Grotesquery's writhing mass of teeth and horns stilled, leaving the clean patch of red stone directly in front of her.

She stared at the book, watching the devils sink back into the mud, until only their dirty eyes blinked up at her.

Hands trembling, she felt like a little girl again, about to touch the book for the first time. 'It's only a scratch,' she murmured, then dug her fingers into the mud and raked them down the cover.

Sharp teeth bit into her skin. She winced but kept scraping. Her hands filled with mud, blood and biting teeth. When they could hold no more she smeared them on the wall.

Tom kneeled beside her. 'You've done it.'

She shook her head. 'I have to do the other side.' Turning the book, she scraped more mud into her hands, screwing her eyes shut as the devils bit again. Though her hands stung, relief welled in her—Mam had been right all along. Their bites were only scratches.

She smeared thick handfuls onto the wall, coating it brown with streaks of red. When all the mud was off the book, the Grotesquery began to turn like a spinning wheel.

'What's it doing?' asked Tom.

'Healing itself,' said Frank.

The book looked smaller without its muddy layer. Through dark stains, Rayne saw the cover was a bright cherry wood. Wishing it had always been that way she carefully rewrapped the cloth and stored the book inside the satchel.

The Grotesquery spun faster and faster. The clear patch of wall had vanished and was replaced with a hundred pairs of bright red eyes. Stubby Nose poked its head through the wall. It looked Rayne up and down, then stretched its face into a wide toothy grin. 'We will not forget thiss.'

A gap opened in the centre, rolling clockwise as it reformed into an arch. The lane became visible again, leading up between the houses. Warily she stepped inside and looked up. The Grotesques were now motionless, their faces stuck like mini statues. 'Did my mother pass this way?'

The faces didn't move.

She and Tom walked out from the shadows into cold sunshine. The arch behind hissed and clicked. Rayne spun around. The red stone writhed and churned anticlockwise. It filled the gap once more, sealing them inside the citadel.

'We have allowed many Sspell Breatherss insside. But we have not sseen your mother. If you find her, tell her we want a word.'

ONWARDS
AND UPWARDS

A cold shiver ran down Rayne's spine. Had she made another mistake? If the Grotesques hadn't seen Mam, then she was still outside the citadel. How could they find her when they were trapped inside?

'Do not worry,' said Frank. 'It is very likely your mother entered the Great Library via a secret way.'

'What makes you say that?' asked Tom.

'Think about it. If you had stolen Grotesques the last time you were here, you would hardly return the same way, would you?'

'Fair point.' Tom dug into his pockets. 'Well, if she is outside, at least the Grotesques will let her in now.' He looked at Rayne. 'She might not be happy you've taken them off her book, though.'

She lifted her chin. 'It got us inside, didn't it? Besides, now anyone can touch it. It'll be easier to repair.'

'Pity,' said Frank. 'I was looking forward to watching Tom trying to restore the book while trying not to lose his fingers.'

The corners of Rayne's mouth twitched as she turned to face the winding cobblestoned lane, rising between a row of tall whitewashed houses. They glinted in the sunshine like Grotesque fangs. A chill wind blew a flurry of dirty parchments and dead leaves down the lane. They rustled around her feet. 'Which way now, Frank? Straight up?'

'Yes, my dear.' He settled his head back on her shoulder. 'In the citadel, all paths lead to the Great Library.'

The wind blew in their faces as they trudged past the first house. They stopped to peer through its broken window. A kitchen table was laid with empty plates and tankards. In the corner lay an overturned chair. Everything was covered in a thick layer of grime. 'What happened to the people?' asked Rayne.

'Looks like they left in a hurry,' said Tom, pointing at a tin bath in front of a blackened hearth. 'It's still full of water.'

Rayne followed his finger and wrinkled her nose; floating on the surface was a thick layer of green scum.

Tom walked to the next house and looked inside. 'It's the same here.'

Glass shattered. Rayne spun round. A smashed window lay in pieces on the ground.

Tom gasped. 'Monsters?'

'Maybe it's Mam, or one of the lost Spell Breathers!' Rayne sprinted across the cobbles towards the glass. Frank's head bounced on her shoulder. She peered through the broken window. Her shoulders slumped. The room was empty.

'Come, let us proceed,' said Frank.

She nodded and walked up the slope, adjusting Frank's position across her shoulders.

'How do you know so much, Frank?' she asked. 'You're a finding Spell, so you'd know about the secret ways, but how come you know about the plague and the Grotesquery?'

'I used to work here.'

'Really? Doing what?'

'Oh this and that, mostly finding lost books and repairing quills for Word Masters.'

'Is that why the finding Spell brought you to us?'

She tucked chilled fingers into his fur. 'I thought it chose you because you were close by. I thought it gave you the power to speak.'

Frank's ears drooped.

'You've always been able to speak, then?'

'Not always like this. How you see me today is the result of a Spell . . . which I received a long time ago.'

'What Spell?' asked Tom.

'It is a rather painful memory. I would rather not discuss it.'

Tom shrugged and walked on. The wind blew colder the higher they climbed. Rayne shivered, wishing she still had her cloak. A sense of loneliness and decay washed over her like a Spell. Everywhere, cobblestones were cracked and broken by thick weeds, doors hung from hinges, and ivy crawled over what had once been people's homes. If they could not save their friends, Penderin would look like this one day.

'What started the plague?' she asked. 'If it was a broken Spell book like in Penderin, why didn't the Word Masters restore it?

'They were overwhelmed. All too quickly they had a hundred books to restore. And in the chaos of people running away, more books were smashed.

Your mother was lucky to escape with hers intact. It is little wonder she chose to protect it with Grotesques.'

'Didn't work though,' said Tom.

Rayne hunched her shoulder.

'Rayne's mother kept her Spell book intact for twelve years. With plague so widespread, that was quite an achievement.'

They passed a storage barn. Beside its gaping door, a wooden crate lay broken. Grimy quills scattered across the cobbles, next to dried splashes of sapphire and ruby ink.

Frank surveyed the debris mournfully. 'Such a waste of beautiful inks.'

'Why the quills? Didn't Word Masters mindwrite their Spells into the books they made?' asked Tom.

'Oh no. Word Masters have no sparks inside them. They cannot mindwrite, nor breathe word-magic. They must handscript, the same as everyone. Everyone except you, Rayne.'

'I can't mindwrite either,' Rayne said.

'You can if you want to,' said Frank.

Rayne shook her head.

They walked around a bend in the lane. Overgrown trees and bushes poked through iron railings, their brown leaves strewn across the ground.

Behind them sat tall houses, three and four storeys high; their roof tiles and door knockers flashed gold.

At the end of the lane, they stopped beside a low stone wall. The wind howled over the top, gusting into their faces. Rayne leaned over the parapet, her hair swirling around her head. A long way down, over jagged rocks and boulders, the sun gleamed on the river as it flowed around the harbour walls. She shivered, glad the parapet was between her and the drop.

She scanned the hazy horizon to the west, searching the pink-grey mists for the Penderin mountains. She hugged herself. 'I thought we'd see our mountain from up here. What d'you think's happening back home?'

Tom shook his head. 'Nothing good.'

'Once your book is restored, it all goes away,' Frank reminded them.

'It won't all go away,' snapped Rayne. 'I wish someone else was a Spell Breather instead of me.'

Tom touched her arm. 'You didn't mean to drop the book. I'm sure they'll forgive you.'

She bit her lip.

Frank raised his head from her shoulder. 'Look behind you.'

They turned. Tom whistled softly.

'I have done as you asked,' said Frank. 'I have

brought you to the Great Library.'

Wide-eyed, Rayne walked into a vast courtyard, triple the size of the orchard back home. It was lined with dead oak trees, made alive again as dark green ivy tangled through their branches. At the centre, constructed of solid red stone, rose a magnificent building. Its shape was symmetrical and precise. Two long rows of arched windows, one above the other, nestled into ornamental walls. A grand staircase led up to a terrace and huge double doors emblazoned in gold with the letters G and L. More golden letters circled the building. Letters of the alphabet and other shapes Rayne didn't know. 'What are they?' she asked, pointing.

'The alphabets of every language in the world,' said Frank.

She looked up to the glass dome. Apart from its tattered flag, the building was clean and gleaming, like it had been washed from top to bottom. 'It's beautiful.'

'I am sorry for the plague,' said Frank. 'If not for that, you would have served your apprenticeship here, like your mother.'

'What was it like, back then?'

Frank's eyes shone. 'A place of culture and learning. A time of enlightenment. The Great Library was home to hundreds of people: Spell Breathers, apprentices, citadel officials, Word Masters, an army of servants . . .'

Rayne pictured a bustling square, filled with busy people, some of them carrying cherry wood books and wearing red cloaks.

'It's hard to believe,' said Tom. 'I mean, it's so quiet now.'

They walked towards the sweeping staircase. The double doors towered over them, their gold letters shining in the sunshine. Rayne noticed a smaller, person-sized door cut into one of the larger doors. It creaked and swayed inwards as the wind blew against it.

Tom raised his eyebrows. 'It's open? That's a bit of luck.'

They jogged up the staircase.

'Do not be so quick to judge,' said Frank. 'Once we are inside, focus only on finding the Master Book and the correct bottle of ink. Keep your eyes and ears open and talk only in whispers.'

Rayne shivered. 'Mam said the library was crawling with monsters.'

'That was true twelve years ago. We do not know what lies before us now. Let us not invite trouble this time.'

Remembering the fish-monster camp, Rayne drew a steadying breath and stepped up to the door. Smoothing one hand into Frank's fur, she lifted the other to the sun-warmed wood and pushed.

The door creaked open.

Tom crowded close and they peered inside.

A gilt staircase with a red carpet graced a cavernous entrance hall. Behind the stairs gleamed gilded corridors. Rayne blinked up at the ceiling, where gold letters shone like stars in a sapphire night sky.

A silent hush greeted them. The great hall was empty.

'No monsters,' said Tom, stepping over the threshold. His footsteps echoed on the floor. 'That's got to be lucky.'

Rayne followed, her eyes feasting on the black and white marble floor and sumptuous tapestries hanging against the walls like heavy curtains.

'What's that?' she asked, pointing to where a stream of sunshine lit a large spiral etched into the floor tiles.

Frank's tail twitched. 'Do not concern yourself, my dear. We are here only for the Master Book and the ink.'

'And finding Mam,' she reminded him.

'Quite so,' said Frank.

Tom spun around on the spot. 'How is this possible?'

'How's what possible?' asked Rayne.

'The place is spotless. How come it's so clean? Everywhere outside is falling to bits.'

Rayne looked down; The floor gleamed under her dirty boots.

'The Spell of Cleanliness,' said Frank. 'It was breathed over the public areas and living quarters when the Great Library was first built.'

Keeping her eyes on the floor, Rayne walked towards the wall. One by one her dusty footprints vanished. 'The floor is cleaning itself!'

Tom curled a lip. 'There's a Spell for cleaning?'

'Of course,' said Frank. 'Why spend time cleaning when there are books to read and Spells to craft?'

Rayne grinned and turned to inspect one of the tapestries. It was an embroidered map. At its middle, with a river looping around, was a replica of the citadel. Sewn around that in all directions were tiny clusters of houses and farms. Each had names embroidered under them, names she'd never heard before. She peered at the houses. They were all ruins.

She gasped. 'Tom, come look at the map. Frank was right.'

'Indubitably,' murmured Frank.

Tom came up behind her and frowned. 'They can't all be ruins, can they?' Quickly he traced his finger along the river, back to Penderin.

'That won't work,' said Rayne. 'The warden told me the village isn't visible on any map.'

Tom's finger reached an image of white capped mountains. Right beside the river was a faint image of thatched rooves lined around a village square. Underneath, embroidered letters spelled the name PENDERIN.

'How can that be?' she said.

Tom shrugged. 'Perhaps the magic in the barrier changed when you broke the book?'

She peered closer. The village was circled with a shadow. A line intersected the perimeter at the top. 'What's that?'

'Tom's tunnel,' said Frank.

'Oh yes,' Tom said, almost puffing out his chest.

'This is a living map. Every map in the Great Library is the same. Any change to the world outside is reflected here.' Frank coughed delicately. 'The tunnel was the reason I was able to find Penderin.'

Rayne shot a look at Tom, an idea beginning to fizz in her brain 'When did you finish digging the tunnel?'

'I told you. After school when everyone was in the orchard.'

The idea erupted like a volcano. 'You *idiot!* Your tunnel must be how the stranger on the bridge found Penderin.'

Tom stepped back. 'I don't see how.'

'Keep your voices down,' murmured Frank.

'It must be that, because I hadn't dropped the book then,' Rayne hissed. 'All this time I thought the plague was my fault. But you're just as much to blame as me. Your stupid tunnel started everything! If you hadn't dug it the stranger wouldn't have shown up and Mam would never have left.'

'Hey. You can't put this on me. I'm not the one who threw her mother's Spell book on the fire.'

She thumped her hands on her hips. 'It slipped.'

Tom folded his arms.

'Look. If Mam hadn't left, I would never have held it over the fire in the first place, and everybody would be fine.'

'And I would still have my bones,' Frank reminded them.

Tom's arms fell by his sides. 'If my tunnel is the cause of this, I'm sorry.'

Anger and relief at having someone else to blame fought inside her. 'Oh don't worry. I'm sure everyone back home will *understand*. I'm sure they'll *forgive you.*'

'Why should they forgive *me*?' He jabbed his finger. 'You're their Spell Breather. It's *your* job to protect them.'

Rayne's head jerked back, like she'd been slapped. 'No Tom, that's Mam's job, and because of you she left me. Just because you can't wait to leave your parents, doesn't mean I feel the same way.'

'Leave them out of this.'

'Why? Two days ago you didn't care if running away would make them sick with worry.'

'That's not true.' Tom trembled. 'I care so much I dug the tunnel to prove they don't have to live off Spells!'

'Well, congratulations. With Mam gone, there are no more Spells.' She scrunched her hands into fists. 'Do you think everyone is better off now?'

Tom frowned and looked away.

She stepped forward. '*Do you*?'

'Frank, where is this Scriptorium?' Tom asked, quietly.

'Why?'

'Because I'm going to take the Spell book there. You two can find the Master Book without me.'

Frank whined. 'It will be safer if we stay together

as we planned.'

'Safer from what? The place is empty. No monsters, no Spell Breathers. Nothing.'

'Yes, you go,' said Rayne. 'Just don't go digging any tunnels while you're about it.'

Frank looked from one to the other and sighed. 'Very well.' He nodded towards the left-hand passage behind the grand staircase. 'You will find the Scriptorium at the end of the corridor. We will join you shortly.'

Tom turned on his heel and walked towards the corridor.

'This is a bad idea,' said Frank. 'Call him back.'

'My best friend caused my worst nightmare.' She turned back to the map. 'We're better off without him.'

16

SILENCE IN
THE GREAT LIBRARY

Tom's footsteps faded. The silent hush returned, along with Rayne's guilty thoughts. He was right, in Mam's absence she *was* supposed to protect the village. She looked down at her boots. If only she hadn't been born a Spell Breather, everyone would be fine now. She sighed deeply. 'Where do we find this Master Book of yours?'

'In the Dictionary Room, up the staircase.'

She crossed to the stairs and bounded up them, two at a time, pausing at the top to look down a long corridor. Overhead, beams of sunshine shone from skylights, creating a patchwork of light and dark on the red carpet. On either side, cherry wood doors edged in gold filigree hid their secrets.

'Which one is it?'

'The double doors at the end,' said Frank. 'At the heart of the Great Library.'

Rayne hastened down the corridor. *Please let me find Mam in the Dictionary Room.*

Two spots of golden light gleamed up ahead. The Dictionary Room's door handles seemed to shine a welcome. With each step, they glowed more brightly, fuelling a growing hope Mam would be waiting.

As she got close, she saw their faces reflected in the wood; hers smiling and eager, and Frank's eyes wide, staring intently. Across her shoulders, she felt his tail and head quiver.

'Don't worry, Frank. You'll soon have your bones back.'

She reached the doors and grasped their golden handles. Twisting them, her heart skipped a beat as they swung open, revealing an enormous sun-drenched chamber.

'Mam?' Her voice echoed across the room.

Frank craned his head to look around the back of the doors. He stopped trembling. 'She is not here.'

Rayne's gaze swept the room. It was the largest she'd ever seen, almost as big as the village square.

The walls glowed with cherry wood bookcases, stretching from a red carpet to the gleaming glass dome. Golden ladders lay propped against bookshelves and golden letters blazed on each crest. Every row shone with gold-covered books.

She stepped further inside. 'It's beautiful.'

Disappointment at not finding Mam slid from her shoulders like a heavy cloak. She spun around slowly. 'There must be thousands of books in here.'

'You see now why Word Masters are necessary for the creation of Spells. There are an extraordinary number of words in this room. No Spell Breather could ever hope to remember them.'

She walked towards a lofty bookcase and inspected a row of gleaming books. She plucked one from the shelf. A golden D shimmered on its cover. Opening a page, she breathed in the scent of cinnamon and beeswax.

She ran her finger down a list of words.

Dedicate

Delicate

Delicious

Delight

Depend

Deserve

Written in neat handscript under each word was a lengthy paragraph of text. 'This doesn't look like a normal dictionary,' she said.

'Far from it. The first sentence describes the word's meaning. The rest describes the word's magic, and its effect when blended with other words to form a Spell. Different blends create different strengths of magic.'

'Like different ingredients create different flavours?'

'Yes, that is a good analogy.'

She slotted the book back into place and skimmed her fingers across the spines, hoping to feel a tingle of word-magic. It was a silly thought, she knew these books weren't Spells, but she liked how they reminded her of Mam.

'You will find the Master Book in the centre of the room,' said Frank.

She walked between long rows of reading tables laden with heavy books. Their ruby, emerald, and sapphire studded covers glowed in the sunlight streaming through the glass dome. Directly in the centre of the chamber rose a tall lectern. On its slanted shelf lay a cherry wood book, exactly the same size as Mam's Spell book.

A soft voice called out. 'There you are. I've been

looking everywhere for you.'

Rayne turned. A powerful surge of joy tore through her, far stronger than any Spell. A huge smile swept across her face. Everything was all right now. '*Mam.*'

She stood in the doorway. Her red cloak around her shoulders and her dark braids wrapped about her head. A familiar smile lit her face.

Rayne launched herself across the room, arms outstretched, longing to be folded inside a hug. 'I've missed you so much.'

Mam's hands stayed by her sides. Frown lines appeared around her eyes.

Rayne stumbled to a walk. 'Please don't be angry. We've come to help you make things better.'

Mam tilted her head to one side.

Rayne stopped still. Confused, she dropped her arms. 'Mam?'

'I wish you'd stop calling me that. I am not your mother.'

Rayne staggered. Not Mam? The woman was her mirror image. Rayne studied her face. There *were* subtle differences. Her eyes had dark circles under them. Her lips were thinner than Mam's. 'Who are you?'

The woman smiled brightly. 'My name is Mali.

You may call me Auntie Mali.'

Rayne blinked. 'Mam's got a sister?'

Mali sighed and walked into the room. 'Didn't she tell you about me?' She put a hand on her hip and pulled at her earlobe. 'Well, I can't say I'm surprised. We didn't part on the best of terms. No matter. It's time you and I got to know each other.'

'Isn't Mam here?'

Mali frowned. 'No. Isn't she with you?'

'We're looking for her. She said she was coming here.'

'Maybe she's on her way, then.'

'I hope so. Frank says there are many secret ways into the library.'

'And who is Frank?'

Rayne gestured to the fox on her shoulder. 'This is Frank. He guided me and T—'

'Very pleased to meet you,' Frank interrupted. 'Even though Rayne has yet to find her mother, it is most welcome news she has found an aunt.'

Mali shot him a questioning look, then smiled. 'Rayne, is it? Well now. I am pleased Meleri named you Rayne. Did you know that was your grandmother's name?'

Rayne shook her head, wondering what other of Mam's secrets Mali had to share.

Mali walked closer. 'I feel like I've had the Spell of Luck breathed over me. I've been searching for you and your mother for years, ever since the plague struck and we lost each other.' She bent forwards and hugged Rayne. 'Aw, it does my heart good to see you.'

Even though she knew it wasn't Mam, her aunt's arms were warm and comforting. Rayne melted into her embrace. Frank slipped from her shoulders and landed in a heap on the carpet.

She broke free and picked him up. He was trembling again. 'Sorry,' she whispered.

Mali guided them towards two red velvet sofas positioned beside a gold crested mantelpiece.

'You were here when the monster plague began?' asked Rayne.

Mali nodded. 'It started in the assembly hall, during your mother's graduation. I only knew something was wrong when people started screaming. The lady next to me, her legs melded together.' She shuddered at the memory. 'It was awful the way bits of material from her skirt stuck out of her swollen leg.'

Rayne cringed, remembering the way Old Flo's neck had sprouted out of her shawl.

'Everyone who was able ran for their lives,' continued Mali. 'I stayed and looked after the people who couldn't look after themselves. Sadly they're all gone now.'

Rayne's blood ran cold.

Mali squeezed her shoulder. 'Come and sit down, you must be tired after coming all the way from . . . Penderin, is it?' Mali sat on the sofa and patted the seat next to her.

'You know about Penderin?' Rayne asked. She lay Frank on the opposite sofa and sat beside her aunt.

'Well, I searched everywhere else for Meleri. When your village popped up on the living map in my study I hoped she might be there. Before then, the map had shown nothing but pine forests. I was preparing to journey to Penderin when you arrived.'

Rayne pursed her lips. Next time Tom said his tunnel hadn't done any harm, she'd steal his shovel and bang him over the head with it.

Mali patted Rayne's hand. 'You must have a hundred questions.'

She had a thousand questions. Whenever she'd asked Mam about her family, Mam had always said there was no one else. 'Are you a Spell Breather too?'

'Goodness no.' Mali smiled thinly. 'Spell Breathers only have one magic spark to pass on. Our mother's spark went to Meleri, not me.'

Rayne sighed. 'You're lucky. I don't want to be a

Spell Breather. And now Frank says me and Mam are the last ones.'

Mali frowned. 'The last ones?'

'I told Rayne about the missing Spell Breathers,' explained Frank. 'How they came here and were never seen again.'

'Oh those old stories,' said Mali, her brow clearing. 'I've been living here for years, and I can tell you they're not here.'

'If they're not here. Where are they?'

Mali shrugged and then smiled at Rayne. 'Let me ask you a question. What brings you to the Great Library? I know you're looking for your mother, but what I don't know is why?'

A flush stole up Rayne's neck. 'Two days ago, I broke Mam's Spell book.'

'You did *what?*'

'It was an accident,' she said, cringing.

'I'm sure it was.' Mali leaned forward. 'So that's why Meleri came here? To find her bottle of ink and restore her Spells?'

Rayne shook her head. 'Mam left before the book broke. We brought her Spell book here.'

'It is in the Scriptorium waiting for repair,' said Frank. 'We came up here for the Master Book.'

Mali frowned. 'But I don't understand. Why did

my sister leave Penderin in the first place?'

'She wouldn't say.'

Mali looked up through the glass dome, to the black birds circling the ragged flag. 'I don't like it, she should be here by now. Something must be wrong.'

Rayne shivered.

'Don't worry,' Mali squeezed Rayne's hand. 'Now we've found each other, we can find her together.'

A heavy weight lifted off Rayne's chest. She hadn't found Mam, but she'd found the next best thing. 'Where do you think she is?'

'She could be anywhere. I've heard tales of bird-monsters living in the mountains behind Penderin. I heard their broken Spells changed them into winged creatures with feathers . . . and sharp claws.'

'*Claws?*' Rayne jumped to her feet.

Mali grasped both of Rayne's hands. 'Don't worry. I know a way to find her. But I can't do it on my own. Will you help me?'

Rayne returned her grasp. 'Of course, just tell me what to do.'

'Wait a moment. You don't know what I'm asking of you yet.'

The birds outside shrieked and their dark shadows skimmed across the carpet. 'I'll do anything! What do you need?'

'What we need is the Spell of Summoning. If you mindwrite the Spell and breathe it over a living map, wherever your mother is, she will appear before us.'

'But I can't mindwrite!' She glanced up at the birds. 'Isn't there another way?'

Mali sat back. 'Well . . . if you can't, I suppose I could.'

'How? You're not a Spell Breather.'

'No, but I can be. All you've got to do is lend me your magic spark.' Mali leaned closer, a keen eagerness in her eyes. 'We are family. We share the same blood. If you transfer your spark to me, then *I* will become a Spell Breather.'

SPARK LIGHT

Rayne stared at Mali. 'I can give my spark away?'

'Yes, provided you have the knowhow,' said Mali. 'I'm sure Frank will explain everything.'

Frank nodded. 'Remember I said Word Masters used a siphon to remove a sample of a Spell Breather's ink? Well, the siphon can also be used to remove their magic spark. Of course, in the past to have one's spark removed was deemed a punishment.'

'A punishment? Why?'

'Oh, because of all that nonsense about only copying Spells from books,' said Mali. 'Can you believe it? Any Spell Breather who dared mindwrite a thought of their own was considered dangerous and had their spark confiscated.'

'Copying is not nonsense,' Frank murmured.

Mali held up her hand. 'The important thing is, if you want to lend your spark to me, you can. I have the siphon downstairs in my study.'

Rayne's hand stole across her stomach. She'd always longed for someone else to be the village Spell Breather, but the spark was her last link to Mam. Before giving it away she had to be sure it would work. She didn't want to make another mistake.

'Where is the Spell of Summoning?' she asked, letting go of Mali's hand. 'Is it in the Master Book?'

'No. That's a book for everyday Spells. The one we want is special. I'll show you.'

Rayne's feet left the ground and she soared towards the glass dome, her arms flailing. *'Help!'*

'Don't worry, I've got you,' said Mali.

Rayne shot Mali a look. Her left hand was raised in the air and she was flicking her fingers sideways. As if in response, Rayne glided across the chamber.

'What are you doing?' she gasped.

Mali beamed a wide smile. 'Showing you the summoning Spell. Now hold still, while I lower you down, or you might hurt yourself.'

Rayne landed softly beside a reading table. She gripped its edges, panting. 'How did . . . you do that?'

Mali shrugged. 'I have some small magic at my

disposal. I can move people, or parts of their bodies, at will. It was a gift from your mother.'

Rayne's eyes stretched wide. 'I didn't know Spells could give people magic powers?'

'Usually they can't. But this was a rather special Spell.'

'Can you use your magic to bring Mam here?'

'I would if I could, but the Spell your mother breathed over me had limits. I must know where a person is before I am able to control them.'

If Mam had given her sister magical abilities, they must have been very close. If she lent her spark to Mali, she was sure to summon Mam in a heartbeat.

On the reading table lay a thick book. It was edged with gold and encrusted with bright gems. Its pages crackled as Rayne turned them back and forth. Her eyes began to glow as she read the different Spells, handwritten in ordinary black ink.

The Spell of Dream walking
The Spell of Shapeshifting
The Spell of Omniscience
The Spell of Endurance
The Spell of Time sliding

Each margin glowed with tiny people enacting the Spells. None of them were monsters. If Tom were to see these he'd change his mind about having a Spell breathed over him.

She found the summoning Spell.

ᘓ THE SPELL OF SUMMONING ᘔ

O rder and invoke
Convene and convoke
Assemble and arise
Manifest, materialize
Your presence, I command
Come _____, I demand

It was exactly the kind of Spell that could bring Mam to her. But she could never mindwrite it herself. Even if they siphoned all her ink, she didn't have a clue how to copy it.

Mali came to stand beside her. 'You see how powerful it is? We only need to add Meleri's name at the end and it will bring her straight to us.'

Rayne nodded. 'So how would you mindwrite the Spell? Will you siphon your ink, so you can copy the Spell, like Mam?'

'There's no time. Your mother might be in

trouble. I will mindwrite the pure way.'

'What does that mean?'

'Instead of copying a Spell, I must create it fresh in my mind. And I do that by focusing on each word, its true meaning, and the outcome I want.'

'What if you spell the words wrong or forget one of them?'

'I won't. Once the words are secured to the parchment, I will check them before I breathe the Spell free.'

'But what if—'

'Stop worrying.' Mali closed the book and hefted it off the table. 'I've had lessons you know.'

'Have you? When?'

'When your mother was at apprentice school, she'd often ask me to swap places with her, so she could sneak off on the weekends. No one ever guessed we'd switched. I may not have breathed any actual Spells, but I know all the theory.'

She walked towards the double doors. 'Come down to my study. I'll show you the spark siphon. You can decide if you want to try the Spell yourself or lend your spark to me.' She reached the door and turned back. 'Let's bring your friend too.'

Mali flicked her fingers and Frank rose from sofa. He floated across the tables towards Rayne, his eyes squeezed shut. Mali draped him across Rayne's shoulders and she settled him more securely. 'Thank you.'

Mali nodded and strode down the corridor. 'Hurry up. We mustn't keep your mother waiting,' she called.

Rayne trailed Mali down the corridor.

'What will you do?' asked Frank.

'I don't know.'

'It would be better if you were to mindwrite the Spell yourself.'

She thought back to her lesson, remembering how the parchment had looked like she'd sneezed over it. 'I'll never be as good as Mam, but Mali will be. You've seen how powerful she is.'

At the top of the grand staircase, she looked down into the hall. Mali was standing next to the spiral in the floor. It looked different. No longer etched into marble, it was now a set of curved steps leading down into darkness.

Rayne ran down the stairs and across to Mali, her boots tapping across the black and white tiles.

Mali gestured to the steps. 'After you.'

Rayne glanced towards the corridor Tom had taken to the Scriptorium. Should she fetch him? She hunched a shoulder and stepped onto the stairs. They didn't need him; Mali could find Mam without him droning on about how people didn't need Spells.

The narrow spiral wound round and down, becoming darker with every step. She leaned against the wall for support. Dust clung to the arm of her tunic. 'What's happened to the cleaning Spell?'

'It was never breathed down here,' said Frank, his voice echoing off the stones.

At the bottom, smoking fire torches flickered light across a dank and mouldy corridor. The smell of damp mixed with soot wafted up Rayne's nose. She peered into the gloom. A door led off to the left and another to the right. The corridor ended abruptly at a rusting portcullis. The black emptiness beyond made her shiver.

Mali trotted down the stairs. 'It's not as grand as upstairs, but I like it. All the best books are kept down here.'

'Which door is your study?' asked Rayne.

'On the right.'

Rayne walked forwards. The sound of stone scraping stone made her turn back. The steps were spiralling inwards and upwards. They locked together in the ceiling with a sharp click.

Mali strode past. 'It gets very draughty down here. So I like to keep it closed.' She turned into her study. 'Here we are.'

Rayne followed her inside. The room was small. A desk, a chair, and a narrow bench huddled against a cobwebbed wall. Over her shoulder, she saw shelves of books bound in a mix of cherry wood and black leather. The top shelf housed a collection of glass jars filled with water and small white somethings. She peered at them. 'Are those bones?'

'Hmm? Oh, yes.' Mali thumped the book on her desk. 'Quaint, aren't they?'

On a wall to her right hung a tapestry map; its bright threads glowed in the candlelight.

'It's not as large as the one in the hall, but you can see it covers the land between here and your home,' said Mali. 'I'm sure once the Spell is breathed over it, your mother will step right out of the map.'

She opened a drawer and brought out a silver box. 'Here is the siphon.' She flipped open the lid. Inside on a bed of red silk lay a delicate glass cone the size of a tankard. Attached to the pointed end was a silver tap. 'We must be careful with it. It's one of a kind.'

'How does it work?'

'Very simply. Twist the tap right for ink and left for a spark.' She laid the box on the desk. 'So, do you want to give the Spell a try? Or will you lend your spark to me?'

From her shoulder Frank blinked steadily up at her. She looked at the map, wishing Mam was here to tell her what to do.

Mali sighed. 'You said yourself, you don't want to be a Spell Breather. And I don't blame you, it's a big responsibility. Best not to try if you think you'll make a mistake.' She put her arm around Rayne's shoulder and squeezed. 'I'm sure your mother would say the same . . . if she was here.'

Mali's voice sounded just like Mam's.

'And I only want to borrow your spark. I'll give it back to you, I promise. Then, when it's all over, you can restore your book and go home.'

Rayne's eyes pricked with tears. She wanted that above all things. She needed Mam. She couldn't save the villagers without her. Auntie Mali could summon her. All she needed was a spark. Slowly, she slid Frank from her shoulders and stretched him out on the desk. 'What do you want me to do?'

'Good girl! Lie on the bench. We'll soon have your mother here.'

The bench was too small to lie flat, so Rayne squashed herself in between its wooden armrests. Mali stood over her holding the cone. 'Now, hold still. According to the books this won't hurt at all.'

Rayne glanced at Frank. He stared at her but said nothing.

Mali pressed the open end of the cone onto Rayne's midriff and twisted the tap to the left. It made a grinding noise as she screwed it anti-clockwise. Through her tunic Rayne felt the rim of the glass grow hot. A bright glow filled the cone. She realized with a shock that the light was coming out of her body. The glass became hotter as Mali turned the tap again and again. She squeezed her eyes shut, not sure she could stand the heat. She cried out as a sudden pinch jabbed her skin. Immediately the heat subsided. Her eyes flew open and she gasped.

A brilliant speck of light hovered inside the cone.

A golden flare, pulsing with indigo. The most beautiful thing she'd ever seen.

She reached out, wanting to hold it. But Mali pulled the cone away.

She whimpered, because all at once she knew; she'd lost a part of herself. A very important part.

Mali tipped the cone sideways and cradled the spark in her palm. Its golden light reflected in her eyes. '*At last,*' she whispered.

Rayne sat up weakly, rubbing her middle, sure it must be bruised. 'Just a lend, you said.'

Mali's shoulders shook. 'Did I say that?' She

giggled. 'How trusting you are. Just like your mother.'

'What do you mean?' Rayne tried to stand, but her knees buckled, and she slumped down.

Mali put the siphon on the desk. 'Well . . . I may have told one or two untruths just now.'

'Untruths?' Rayne frowned. 'You'll mindwrite the summoning Spell now, won't you?'

Mali began to laugh. 'Ah, you've caught me out, that was a lie.'

Rayne's blood ran cold. She pushed herself up and tried to snatch her spark.

Mali stepped back. 'Oh no you don't. I've waited my whole life for this. I'm not giving it up now.' In one quick movement, she raised the spark to her lips, opened her mouth and tipped it inside. A shaft of light shone out of her mouth, then winked out as she closed her lips and swallowed. 'Mmmm. Delicious,' she purred, rubbing her stomach.

'What are you doing?'

'Taking what's rightfully mine!'

Rayne staggered to her feet. Her insides felt hollow. Distraught she'd lost her last link to Mam, she lunged for the siphon.

Mali flicked her fingers.

With a will of their own Rayne's hands balled into fists and punched the siphon off the desk. It crashed to the floor, smashing into hundreds of jagged pieces.

Mali laughed. 'You just can't stop breaking things, can you?'

Rayne fell to her knees. 'Noooo!'

TREACHERY

Rayne's hands fluttered over the broken shards. 'How will I get my spark back now?' she howled.

'Haven't you been listening to me?' Mali loomed over her. 'You won't ever get it back.'

Rayne looked up and recoiled. Mali might have Mam's face, but it was twisted with greed and hatred. She'd been stupid to trust her. Mali might not have the plague, but she *was* a monster. The worst of all. Rayne ground her teeth. 'Mam must hate you very much.'

'Hate? She doesn't know the meaning of the word.' Mali sneered. She glanced at the tapestry map. 'But wherever she is, I suspect she's beginning to. Soon she'll understand it completely!'

Rayne got to her feet. Her legs wobbled. 'What

do you mean?'

Mali smirked. 'Why do you think she hid you behind her barrier?'

'To protect us from the plague,' Rayne said, but part of her wasn't so sure now.

'From the plague,' mimicked Mali. 'Rubbish. She could've breathed a hundred different Spells for that. No, it was to hide your magic sparks from *me*.'

Rayne gasped.

Mali rubbed her stomach. 'And I'm so very glad I got yours and not my sister's. Yours hasn't been sullied by that disgusting charity slop she likes to dish out.'

'*Why are you doing this?* You're Mam's sister, you should be helping her!'

Mali shoved her face close to Rayne's. 'Should? Should!' A drop of spit struck Rayne's chin. 'Don't talk to me about should. I'm the one who should have had our mother's spark.'

Rayne stood her ground. 'If Mam was here she'd stop you.'

Mali stood back. 'Wrong again, little fool. Your mother *is* here.' She swished her red cloak. 'Don't you recognize my cloak? Now you've made me a Spell Breather, my precious sister's going to feel the sharp breath of my power.'

Rayne gaped at the cloak. It did look just like Mam's. A wave of fear tumbled over her. 'Where is she?'

Mali flexed the fingers of her left hand. 'Close at hand.' She threw back her head and gave a peal of laughter. 'What a marvellous family reunion this is. Don't you agree, Frank?'

On the desk, Frank looked up at Mali, his amber eyes narrowed to slits. 'Are you satisfied?'

'Delighted.' She bent her head in a mocking manner. 'As usual, you have served me . . . adequately.'

Rayne stared at Frank and then back to Mali. What were they talking about?

Frank bared his teeth. 'Do not keep me waiting.'

'Oh very well.' Mali flicked her fingers and a jar of bones on the bookcase rattled.

Frank shuddered. He growled deeply in the back of his throat. His body and legs began to thicken. He sprang onto his paws and stretched his long back, shaking himself like a dog.

Rayne sat on the bench with a thump. No, it couldn't be.

'You did not need to take my bones, Mali. I thought we trusted one another,' Frank said.

'Do not speak to me of trust!' Mali crooked her finger towards him. 'Finding you in the Dictionary Room wasn't part of our plan. You were supposed to bring her straight down here. Staunch reported you'd passed the Grotesquery an hour ago.'

Frank cringed and lowered his eyes.

Their words sliced through Rayne like a knife. She covered her mouth. Tom had been right not to trust Frank from the start. She'd been so desperate to find Mam she'd walked right into a trap.

Frank sprang from the desk and landed on the bench. He looked up at Rayne with sad eyes. 'I am sorry.'

'Frank. You're my friend.' She reached out her hand. 'You can't be working for *her* . . . you can't be.'

'How touching,' scoffed Mali.

Frank shied away. 'I have no friends.'

Rayne closed her eyes and saw herself back beside the barrier, breathing free the words of the Spell of Finding. She began to tremble. 'I don't believe it. I breathed the Spell from the parchment. You came to me.'

'Your broken word-magic landed on a tree.'

'I didn't take your bones?'

Frank's ears drooped. 'I pretended you did so you would feel pity and allow me to escort you here. You see, once the tunnel was open and Penderin appeared on the living maps, Mali sent me to investigate.'

Rayne wished Tom had never dug his stupid tunnel.

Mali swished her cloak again 'And what did he find when he arrived? You! I said I must have had the Spell of Luck breathed over me, didn't I? Double good luck as it turned out. If you hadn't broken your mother's Spells, she might have got the better of me.' Her smile glittered. 'As it was, when she got here, I had the upper hand.'

Frank hung his head.

The knife twisted in Rayne's stomach. It wasn't all Tom's fault. She was the one who'd turned her friends into monsters, and given away her magic spark, and worst of all . . . she squeezed her eyes shut. Worst of all she'd put Mam in danger.

'I really must thank you for all you've done,' said Mali. 'All the years I've spent searching for your mother, I should have just put my feet up and waited for you to deliver her to me.' Mali tucked Rayne's hair behind her ears. 'Now be a good girl and keep out of my sight. After I've given my sister a taste of her own medicine, I will allow you to remain with me. You won't wish to go back to Penderin. Not now you've turned everyone into monsters.'

Rayne jumped to her feet and bolted for the door. If Mam was close by she had to find her.

Mali flicked her fingers. Rayne froze, mid stride. Every muscle strained to move, but she was locked inside a wall of ice.

Mali laughed. 'Dear me, haven't you learned yet?

You're mine now. I own you.' She folded her arms and walked around Rayne, a smirk playing about the corners of her mouth. 'Just like your mother, always running away.'

Rayne's eyes flashed.

'Don't worry,' Mali purred. 'I've only given you a tiny taste of my power. You'll be walking about soon enough. Now, stay here and behave yourself.' She spun on her heel and stalked into the corridor.

Frank sprang from the bench and trotted close; his eyes glistened 'Forgive me. I had hoped we would restore the Spell book . . .' He dropped his voice to a whisper, 'and you and Tom would have escaped before she found us.'

'*Frank!* Get out here,' screamed Mali. 'Now you're back it's time you smartened yourself up. I have work for you.'

Frank padded to the door, then turned. 'Thank you for saving my life, my dear. But you should have left me at the bottom of the river.' He dropped his gaze and scampered from the room.

Rayne's mind whirled. She urged herself to think of a way to escape. But her thoughts were as stuck as her body. Her vision misted with unshed tears. They blinded her as they clung to her eyes, unable to fall.

WORDS WITH THE
POWER TO HURT ME

Rayne tried to break free. Energy charged through her muscles. She was sprinting, but her body was rigid. Her thoughts raced, unfettered. Why hadn't Mam told her about Mali? Why had she never told her about her spark?

A tingle raced across her face, unfreezing her tears. They slid down her cheeks and fell to the floor. Mam had kept her in the dark because she knew the truth; *her daughter would only mess things up*. And Mam was right. Putting her trust in Mali had been an appalling mistake.

Frank had—her heart burned—*betrayed* her. If she

could have moved her mouth, she'd have howled in frustration. If only she'd listened to Tom instead of arguing with him. She hoped he'd made it to the Scriptorium, hoped he was safe, hoped Mali hadn't trapped him too.

A tingle swept down her arms and legs. Pins and needles bubbled into her feet and she wriggled her toes. Slowly, like wading through freezing water, she put her foot on the floor and straightened up.

She looked at the tapestry map on the wall, studying its embroidered layers, yearning for a real Spell to find Mam. Hot tears welled in her eyes; a Spell couldn't help her now. Without her spark she was just like everyone else. Her mouth turned down at the corners. It used to be all she'd wanted. She rubbed the empty ache in her stomach. Now she wanted her spark back.

Glass shards crunched under her boots. Pieces of the spark siphon lay scattered around Mali's desk. Something silvery glinted in the dust underneath. She peered into the shadow. The siphon's tap gleamed up at her.

She stared at it. Was it really broken? Or was that another of Mali's lies. Reaching for the tap, she turned the cold metal over in her hands. If she was going to get back her spark, she'd have to find the truth for herself.

As Rayne tucked the tap into her pocket, the gem-encrusted Spell book on the desk caught her eye. Even if she could get back her spark, she had no clue how to mindwrite a Spell to find Mam. Maybe she didn't need to. Mali had said Mam was close by. Remembering the gleam in her eye, that was probably true. All she had to do was search the rooms nearby.

Rayne trod softly to the door and leaned against its frame, listening. The corridor was quiet. She poked her head out. To the right, the portcullis barred the way. On each side, two flaming torches flickered shadowy light over its iron grate. She hadn't noticed earlier; the bars were raised up just enough for someone to slide under. Between the grills, the room's inky blackness oozed the smell of damp.

To her left, the spiral staircase was locked into the stone ceiling. Mali must still be down here. The corridor beyond stretched into darkness, studded with dots of firelight.

Rayne tiptoed across the passage to the door opposite and turned the handle. It was locked. 'Mam?' she murmured. 'Are you in there?' She put her ear to the door. Nothing stirred.

She scurried down the corridor and shrank

against the wall, directly under the spiral. How had Mali sealed it? It couldn't be magic, she only had the power to control people. Rayne ran the palm of her hand over the smooth wall looking for a lever.

Snatches of muffled conversation reached her ears. Down the corridor, two dots of firelight began to bob. Rayne blinked. Mali was coming back.

Hugging the wall, she edged backwards until her back pressed against the portcullis. A sour smell of mould wafted through the grill, sticking in her throat.

The approaching torches grew brighter. Two seemingly disembodied heads floated beside them, their voices growing louder. One sounded like Mali. The other was deeper.

Rayne's fingers curled into the metal grill. She tugged upwards. It was rusted fast.

Footsteps click-clacked closer.

She had to hide. If Mali froze her again, she'd never find Mam.

Dropping to the floor, she wriggled under the grate. Its metal spikes raked down her back like claws. Twisting onto her bottom, she pulled her feet inside, just as Mali walked under the spiral into a pool of firelight.

Beside her was a young man with red hair. He wore a long cream robe tied at the waist. It was richly embroidered with golden quills that gleamed in the firelight.

'Come into my study while I'll tell you what I want. And pay attention this time,' Mali snapped. She turned in through the door. 'Ah, my niece has unfrozen. Pity, I wanted her to hear this.'

Rayne shrank into the shadows.

The man shot a searching glance at the portcullis, then hurried inside. The study door scraped along the floor and banged shut.

Rayne got to her feet and shivered. The fetid air was cold and somewhere close by was the slow drip-drip of water.

Orange light filtered through the grill, outlining shadowy bookcases arranged in two half circles facing each other. Like the shelves in the Dictionary Room, each was filled with books, but unlike that sunlit chamber, nothing glowed. The bookcases were covered in mould and grime. Long skeins of spider webs draped across them like ghosts.

She was about to step inside the circle when she heard stone scraping against stone. Darting beside the entrance, she peeked through the portcullis. The spiral staircase was open. Heavy footsteps clomped down their shadowy steps. A shiny bald head emerged into the firelight, followed by the giant body of a man. His sleeveless tunic revealed enormous muscle-bound arms covered in hard black shells. Rayne gaped. At the end of his right arm was a huge, crab-like pincer. It clicked ominously.

The crab-man opened the door to Mali's study.

'There you are, Staunch,' said Mali.

His deep voice rumbled, 'Yes, mistress.'

'Don't dawdle. Now you're here I want you to keep an eye on—'

The door scraped shut.

Rayne crossed her fingers, hoping the person Mali wanted to keep an eye on wasn't Tom. She didn't like the way Staunch reminded her of the fish-monsters.

She crept into the circle of books, noticing small paw prints scattered across the dusty floor. Traitor Frank had been here.

Each bookcase was crested with a different letter of the alphabet, but the shelves were rotting and crammed with black books. Stopping beside a bookcase marked with the letter D, she picked up a dirty tome. A chain rattled out from the shelf, as loud as the blacksmith's hammer. She cringed and shot a look at the grill, dreading to see Mali appear with her left hand crooked, ready to freeze her to the spot.

The torches flickered. No shadow crossed their path. She turned to the book. The metal chain was attached to its spine. Every book in the case was chained to the shelf. She opened the cover and nearly gagged at the stink of wet animal skin. Whoever had chained the books had left them to rot.

Raising the page to the meagre light she squinted at the writing. The books looked like dictionaries. She frowned. Why weren't they in the Dictionary Room? She read the list of words.

Despair

Destroy

Devastate

Disaster

Breath caught in her throat. These words must *never* be put into a Spell! She slammed the book shut.

The study door scraped open. 'Stop your blathering! It's time to open the vault and finish what we started,' said Mali.

Light bloomed through the grill as Mali lifted a fire torch from its bracket and stalked towards the portcullis.

Heart pounding, Rayne replaced the dictionary

and silently fed the chain back into the shelf.

'Staunch, open the gate,' commanded Mali.

Rayne stole behind the bookcase and peeped back around. Prints from her boots had mingled with Frank's paw prints in the dust. If Mali saw them, she would catch her.

Staunch's gigantic pincer clamped around the grill and the rusted iron squealed like a pig as it shot into the ceiling. Mali strode in, lifting her torch above her head. She wrinkled her nose. 'This room smells disgusting. Once I've dealt with my sister, I'll breathe a cleaning Spell in here.'

Rayne shrank into a corner. Jagged stones snagged her back as she pressed against the wall.

The man in the long robe followed Mali inside and walked into the circle of books. His hem swept away the footprints. Rayne relaxed a little, then her eyes narrowed as she focused on his face. Something about him stirred a memory.

Mali entered the circle and caressed the black spines. 'What fun I shall have with these,' she purred.

The man hung his head. Mali's sharp eyes raked over him. 'Stop looking like a wet weekend. I thought you'd be happy. The last time we were in here, you and my sister couldn't wait to get your hands on these dictionaries.'

He looked at Mali with sad eyes. 'Time changes people.' The man shook his head. 'I am sorry I ever told you both I had crafted the Spell of Manipulation. I was wrong to do it. And Meleri was wrong to breathe it over your hand.'

Rayne bit her lip. Why had Mam done that?

Mali flicked her fingers and the man's head smacked into a bookcase. 'Silence, Word Master. I don't care how you feel. You will craft my Spells whether you like it or not.'

Rayne's eyes shot wide. Word Master? There weren't supposed to be any left. What was he doing here?

'Staunch, get in here,' called Mali.

The giant crab-man squeezed through the doorway. The shells on his bulging biceps scraped against the wall.

'Now, Word Master,' said Mali. 'Show Staunch which dictionaries you need for my sister's Spell. He will break their chains.'

The Master took a pair of spectacles from a pocket in his robe and put them on. 'These dictionaries are not for the likes of monsters.'

Staunch snapped his claw at the Master. 'Careful I don't cut your tongue out, little man.'

Mali grinned. 'Staunch will take the books. And

don't dare think about double crossing me.' She crooked her finger. 'If your Spell is weak . . . if she doesn't suffer . . .'

The Master's head whacked against the shelf again, knocking his spectacles askew.

'If she doesn't suffer,' repeated Mali, squashing his face into the shelf, 'I promise you . . . *you will.*'

Mali dropped her hand and the Master reeled backwards. He adjusted his glasses, murmuring, 'Yes, mistress.'

'Hurry up!'

The Word Master walked to a bookcase marked with the letter T. A chain rattled as he picked up a book and opened it. Finding the page he wanted, he read the entry. His hands began to shake. 'Mali. For the sake of the friendship we once had. Do not ask me to craft this Spell,' he pleaded. 'It will torment your sister for eternity.'

'Shut up,' she spat. 'It's time she got what's coming to her for stealing my spark. Now, show Staunch the books you need and be quick about it.'

The Master didn't move.

Mali raised her left hand and cocked an eyebrow. 'Do you really want to defy me?'

Slowly, the Word Master walked around the circle, pointing towards different books. His voice shook as he spoke a cocktail of ugly words. 'Bitter. Poison. Despair . . .'

Rayne clamped a hand over her mouth to stop herself crying out. What had she done? Her own spark was inside Mali, and she was going to hurt Mam with it.

ONCE BITTEN,
TWICE SHY

Staunch trailed the Master around the circle, collecting dictionaries and slicing their chains with his black claw. They jangled into the dust with a bang. When he had six books under his arm, the Master removed his spectacles.

'That's all?' asked Mali.

He closed his eyes and nodded.

'Excellent. Staunch, take the dictionaries to the Scriptorium so the Master can work on the Spell.'

Rayne leaned forward. The Scriptorium? Tom was there. If he hadn't been captured, she had to warn him.

The giant hunched his shoulders and squashed

his body back through the doorway.

'Now the siphon is broken, I cannot siphon the ink from your blood,' said the Master.

'Fool. You know I had no intention of copying the Spell. Stop delaying and hurry along with you. I want a final word with my sister.'

Rayne's heart leapt. If Mali was going to Mam, then she was close by.

'Where is she?' asked the Master. 'I would speak with her.'

'After you deliver the Spell,' Mali purred. 'As for where she is?' She tapped the side of her nose. 'Somewhere secret.'

'Secret?' The Master's brows shot up. 'You have imprisoned her in one of the secret ways?'

The smile wiped from Mali's face. 'How would I know where they are? I am not a Word Master like you.'

'As I have explained countless times, the Masters never told us students where the secret ways were hidden.' He put the spectacles in his pocket. 'If you had allowed me to graduate before you—'

'Oh stop your whining,' Mali said. 'You've had the run of the Great Library for years. Haven't you found one yet?'

The Master shrugged. 'I did hear of a secret way

leading from this chamber straight to the Scriptorium. But given how the Word Masters felt about these dictionaries, that always seemed unlikely.'

'You've waited twelve years to tell me this?' She flicked her fingers. The Master jerked to attention. He whipped around to face the door and marched towards it, his arms swinging wildly. He collided with the wall.

Mali giggled. 'Oops.' She directed him out. 'Once you've finished my Spell, you will come back here and look for this secret way.'

Rayne crept from the shadows and watched Mali march the Master down the corridor. Every few steps he careered into the wall. Pity swirled inside her. She shook it off. He was helping Mali hurt Mam.

She wanted to follow Mali. But first she had to warn Tom and find a way to get back her spark. She turned to study the moss-covered walls. If a secret way did exist it might get her to the Scriptorium before Staunch.

Circling the vault, she searched the stones for a hidden entrance. Green gunge stuck to her fingers and she wiped them on her skirt. Exasperated, she leaned against the wall and looked down at her boots. If the passage was secret, she'd never find it.

She blinked at a trail of dusty paw prints. Frank

knew the secret ways. Had he gone to the Scriptorium to trap Tom, like he'd trapped her? She followed his tracks.

They stopped abruptly beside a wall.

She jabbed her fingers into the stones, scraping the mortar in-between. Nothing. She banged her fist on the wall. 'Come on. Open!'

The wall hissed.

She flinched backwards.

A horn poked through the stone. Two eyes topped with thick bushy brows blinked up at her.

'*You!*' said Rayne.

The stubby-nosed Grotesque emerged from the wall, grinning wickedly.

'What are you doing here?' she asked warily.

Two fat arms reached out of the stone and the Grotesque propped its head on its elbows. 'The Great Library iss not a ssafe place. We came to find you.'

'Why?'

'We owe you a favour.'

Hope fluttered in her chest. 'Can you help me find the way out?'

'You're running away?'

'No. I have to get to the Scriptorium.'

Stubby Nose disappeared into the wall.

Her eyes flew over the stones. 'Hey, where've

you gone?'

'Down here.'

Stubby Nose was poking out of a stone by her foot. Crouching beside it, she asked, 'So, how do I get out?'

'Pussh here.'

She reached out, then stopped. 'How do I know you won't bite me?'

Stubby Nose hissed. 'We have no reasson to bite you.'

'It's never stopped you before.'

'Your mother breathed a Sspell on uss! But we are afflicted no longer.'

Hesitatingly she brought her fingers close to the stone. Stubby Nose sank into the wall. Smiling, she pushed her fingers into the stone. The wall slid back, and a welcome breeze wafted over her face. A narrow door led to a staircase spiralling upwards. Crossing her fingers, she stepped inside.

Orange gloom turned pitch black as the wall behind scraped shut. The stench of damp vanished. 'Are you still here?'

'Right besside you, misssy,' said Stubby Nose, close to her ear.

She groped for the steps and clambered up.

'Did you find your mother?'

'No, but she's here. Mali has her trapped.'

'Mali? Your mother told uss sshe tried to ssteal her sspark the day the plague began. Sshe was running from Mali when sshe robbed uss.'

Rayne gritted her teeth. 'Well Mali's got what she wants now. And unless I find a way to get my spark back, she's going to use it to hurt Mam.'

'Your mother will be ssad you losst your sspark.'

She sped up, pushing her hands onto the cold steps. 'So am I.'

'We thought you would be pleassed.' It sounded surprised. 'You never bothered about Sspell Breathing before.'

She thought back to the last month of lessons with Mam. She'd spent most of the time looking out the window. If they ever got home, things would change.

Muscles grumbling and breath coming in quick bursts, she pushed upwards. Ahead a vertical line of brightness pierced the dark. The stairs levelled off. Edging forwards she put her eye to the light to see long rows of wooden desks. On each, stood boxes of feather quills. Behind them, nestled into a series of arches, were shelves lined with small bottles of ink. A rainbow of golds, purples, emeralds, sapphires, and rubies glowed in the sunlight. 'Is this the Scriptorium?'

'Yess.' Stubby Nose's head poked through the wall beside her. 'You'll be on your own again. The panelled wallss cover the sstone. We cannot enter.'

She peered at its earnest face and half smiled. 'Thank you for helping me.'

'We owed you a favour. Now we are even.' Its fangs sucked its lower lip. 'Your mother still owess uss.'

Wondering what Mam would say, she nudged the door. It swung open to the sound of tinkling glass. Easing her head into the room, she whispered, 'Tom?'

She stepped inside. The door clicked behind her. She spun round, wishing she'd asked how to open it again. This side, the door was lined with large bottles of black ink.

She walked between the desks, their worn surfaces spotted with splodges of dried ink. By the window was a low table piled high with cherry wood books. She picked one up. Just like Mam's book, their Spells were missing words. Where were their Spell Breathers? Frank had said they'd come to the Great Library to repair their books. Mali hadn't seen them. Which one was telling the truth?

A hand slid across her mouth. Her heart leapt.

'Shh,' whispered a familiar voice.

She twisted round. 'Tom!' Relief washed through

her. His tunic was ripped at the shoulder and his hair stuck up at crazy angles. 'What happened to you?'

Tom rubbed his hair, making it stick up even more. 'Been hiding from a monster with a massive claw. I tried to give him the slip to warn you, but I couldn't get past. So I came back here, hid your mam's book and hoped you'd show up.'

He looked around. 'Did you bring the Master Book? Where's Frank?'

'You haven't seen him?'

'No, why? He's got the book though, hasn't he? We need it to save everyone.'

Her mouth turned down at the corners. 'It's a long story. There's no time now. The clawed monster is on his way up here.'

He shot a glance at the door leading to the corridor.

'Look, Tom, I'm sorry for what I said about your parents. I was angry. It was me who messed up, not you.'

Tom shook his head. 'No, I'm sorry. It's not your job to look after anyone.' He sighed. 'Everywhere I've been I've seen my tunnel on the living maps. This is my fault.'

'I've made things ten times worse. I've lost my magic spark.'

'You did *what?*'

She reached out her hand. 'You've got to help me get it back.'

Footsteps echoed along the corridor. Tom grabbed her hand. 'Come on.'

They ran towards the shelves of black ink. Tom skidded beside a low cupboard. 'I've been hiding in here.' He yanked open its doors. 'Get in.'

The footsteps echoed louder.

Together they backed into the cupboard. Rayne pulled her knees to her chest and Tom eased the doors shut. Shoulder to shoulder, they stared through a crack in the wood.

Staunch clomped into the Scriptorium, followed by the Master. 'Put the dictionaries on my desk and go.'

The crab-man clattered the books down. 'I've orders to wait until you've finished,' he growled.

'Standing guard over me, Staunch?'

The monster smirked. 'Orders is orders.'

The Master put on his spectacles and opened a black dictionary. 'Ah, I need another dictionary.'

'You said you had them all. She won't be happy if you delay.'

'That cannot be helped. Be a good monster and go back to the vaults. Bring the first book from the shelves marked T.'

Staunch snapped his claw. 'You'd better hurry, little man, or she will make you sorry.'

The Master shrugged. 'She did that a long time ago.'

Staunch grunted and walked into the corridor.

The Master sat at a desk and plucked a quill from a stand. Dipping the quill in a pot of black ink, he began to scratch the Spell. Every few minutes he searched inside the black books, muttered to himself and bent to his work once more. Finally, he removed his spectacles and rubbed his eyes. His chair scraped back. 'More black ink.'

Rayne watched, her eyes widening as his boots advanced towards the shelves of bottled ink above their heads.

The boots stopped.

The bottles clinked.

The Master's knees bent suddenly, and his thin face peered through the crack in the door. A dark bruise shone on his forehead.

'Greetings.' He swept the cupboard doors wide. 'I want to talk to you.'

WHERE THERE'S
A WILL THERE'S A WAY

Rayne and Tom exchanged worried frowns. His shoulder squashed into her as he shuffled out of the cupboard. Heart pounding, she crawled after him.

The Master held out his hands.

'Keep away from us!' said Rayne.

The Master cast an anxious glance at the door. 'Keep your voice down,' he murmured. 'My pincered jailor is not the quickest on two legs. He will be back in fifteen minutes, sooner if he hears you shouting.'

'Who are you?' asked Tom.

'Someone who wants to help.'

Rayne spied the Master's Spell on his desk behind

him, encased in a black leather folder. She sprinted towards it, snatched it up and opened the file.

❧ THE SPELL OF TORMENT ❧
Soul poisoned, bleak
Heart breaking, weak
Gut wrenched distress,
Bitter, lost, hopeless
Mournful despair
Endless nightmare

'You monster!' she gasped. 'How is this helping?'

'Do not call me that.' Pink-cheeked, the Master plucked the folder from her fingers. 'I can help you in other ways.'

'Give it back.' She jumped for it, intent on ripping it to shreds. 'It can't hurt Mam if *she* doesn't have it.'

The Master reached up and put the folder on top of a tall bookcase.

'Why are you helping her?' Rayne demanded.

'Because I have no choice.' The Master prodded the darkening bruise on his temple and winced. 'Last time I disobeyed her she froze me for a year.'

Rayne bit her lip. Being frozen for half an hour had been bad enough.

'Do not blame me,' the Master continued, irritably. '*You* should not have given her your spark.'

'She tricked me into it.' Rayne's eyes narrowed. 'If you hadn't written the Spell of Manipulation for her all those years ago, none of this would be happening at all.'

The Master turned away.

Tom walked up to them, a frown creasing his brow. 'What are you talking about?'

'You're right to be wary of Spells, Tom. Some are dangerous.' She pointed to the stack of black books on the Master's desk. 'See those? They're dictionaries. Before today, they were chained downstairs in the vaults.'

'Why?'

'You heard the Spell he's writing for Mam. Its words are evil.'

Tom reached across to the nearest book and flipped open a page. He ran a finger down its list of words. 'Maim. Malice. Malevolent.' He frowned. 'Who wants to breathe words like this?'

'Mali does,' said the Master.

Tom looked from the Master to Rayne. 'Who's Mali?'

'My aunt.'

'Your what? You're joking!'

Rayne groaned. 'I wish I was. Mali is Mam's twin sister. I didn't know she existed until today. She's not a Spell Breather. At least . . .' Rayne's shoulders sagged. 'She wasn't until I gave her my spark.'

She told him everything then. It tumbled out in one long rush. How Mali had promised she'd find Mam. How her magic had made Rayne smash the spark siphon. And finally, with halting breaths she told him how Mali wanted to use her spark to hurt Mam.

'Where is Frank?' asked Tom. 'Why didn't he help you?'

Hot tears pricked Rayne's eyes. 'I don't know, and I don't care. You were right about him, Tom. All the time he was pretending to be our friend, he was working for Mali.'

The Master sat heavily on a bench and fiddled with his spectacles.

'He's not the Spell of Finding?' asked Tom.

She shook her head. 'He lied.'

Tom sat on the bench beside the Master. 'Well . . . and I was just beginning to like him.'

The Master raised his eyebrows. 'You were?' He folded his arms. 'I do not like him. He is a loathsome creature. She makes him do far worse than me.'

Tom's eyes widened. 'I know you. You're the stranger who tried to enter Penderin. The one

Rayne's mam knocked off our bridge!'

Rayne studied the Master's face. It was the same man, same bushy red hair, only now it hung loosely over his shoulders. 'You know Mam?'

He nodded. 'We were friends. As I wish to be to you.'

'We will never be friends.'

'You say that, but if I had not spoken of the secret way in the vaults just now, you would still be trapped down there.'

Rayne shook her head. 'If you were Mam's friend you wouldn't be doing this to her.'

'Why did you come to Penderin?' asked Tom.

'When your village appeared on the maps Mali sent me to investigate.'

Rayne glared at Tom. He hunched his shoulder and picked up a quill, concentrating on running the fronds between his fingers.

'I was glad the tunnel appeared,' the Master continued. 'I wanted to ask Meleri for help. But as you saw, she would not listen to me.' He sprang up and walked to the stack of tattered Spell books by the window. 'These once belonged to Spell Breathers. Good men and women who used their Spells to help people.'

'Did you want Mam's help to find them?'

The Master caressed the topmost book. 'It is too late for those poor souls.'

Tom and Rayne frowned at each other.

A tear skimmed the Master's cheek. 'Every day I try to make amends by restoring their Spells. The people they looked after, they are monsters now . . .' He swallowed. 'If they found a way to eat and sleep and not become crazed, then restoring these books makes them well again.'

Rayne thought about her friends back home, hearing again their cries for Mam. How long was Old Flo's neck now? How long would it take her to swallow food?

Tom lifted the lid of the nearest desk and brought out Mam's satchel. 'What about our Spell book? Can you repair it?'

The Master wiped his eyes quickly. 'Of course. I said I want to help.' He walked towards the wall of rainbow inks. 'I have Meleri's ink here.' He put his spectacles up to his eyes and selected a bottle of golden ink. He held it aloft. 'See? A beautiful shade of butterscotch.'

He walked back past the tall bookcase, sliding the folder with the Spell of Torment into his hand. 'I will repair your book and help you escape to Penderin.' He put Mam's ink inside her satchel and stared at the folder. 'But I am sorry, first I must deliver Mali's Spell.'

Rayne put her hands over his. 'Don't. *Please.*'

'I have no choice.' He sighed. 'You will come to learn, as I have, Mali always wins.'

'No! There must be another way.' She pulled the siphon tap from her tunic pocket. 'What about this? Can we use it to get my spark back?'

The Master shook his head sadly. 'Without the glass cone it is completely useless.'

Rayne opened her fingers and the silver tap thumped onto the desk. It rolled over the edge and bounced on the floor. She kicked it into a corner.

The Master said gently, 'I thought you did not want to be a Spell Breather?'

'How do you know?' asked Tom.

The Master shrugged. 'Frank told me, before he slunk off.'

'I thought I didn't. But I do now,' said Rayne. 'I'll breathe a thousand Spells if I have to. I'll do *anything* to help Mam.'

'Well then . . .' The Master contemplated Mam's satchel. 'I wonder?' He looked at Rayne. 'Did you know that before we wrote Spells into books we stored them in bottles?'

'Bottles?' repeated Rayne, blankly.

The Master smoothed his beard. 'Yes, bottles.

Spells breathed into glass bottles and sealed before their word-magic could take effect. People used to think Spells could be dispensed like medicine, by anyone, not just Spell Breathers. Unfortunately it was not as simple as that.'

Tom folded his arms. 'There's a surprise.'

The Master's lip turned up at the corner. 'Yes, Tom, your scepticism is well founded. People made mistakes. They used the wrong Spell or too strong a Spell and hurt themselves and others. Without a Spell Breather to direct the word-magic, the ink would sometimes splash over the wrong person.'

'How does this help us?' asked Rayne.

'When I was apprenticed here I overheard the Masters talk of a secret hall, deep in the bowels of the Great Library. A hall filled with blue glass bottles. Inside those bottles writhe words from Spells breathed long ago.'

Tom sat forward. 'What are you saying? The library has a room full of old Spells?'

'That is exactly what I am saying.'

Hope blossomed inside Rayne. 'Where is it? Maybe we can find some Spells to stop Mali.'

'Well, there is the rub,' said the Word Master, stroking his chin again. 'I have been searching the secret ways for many years. I have never found it.'

Tom tutted and sat back.

'Wait a minute.' Rayne bounced on her toes. 'I know how we can find it.'

'How?' asked Tom and the Master in unison.

Muffled thuds and sharp scissoring clicks echoed from the corridor outside.

'Staunch is coming back,' hissed Tom.

KEEPING IT
IN THE FAMILY

The Master tucked the black folder into his belt and beckoned Tom and Rayne. 'Follow me. *Quickly.*'

Tom snatched up Mam's satchel.

'Leave it. We cannot risk damaging the book further.' The Master darted towards a tall book press tucked between two bookcases. Grasping its central wheel, he turned it clockwise. As the wooden paddle screwed up, one of the bookcases slid back revealing a dark passage. 'Get in.'

Tom ran inside. Rayne hesitated. Trusting Frank had been a mistake. Could they trust this Master?

Staunch's footsteps quickened and grew louder.

Deciding to worry about it later she rushed inside and pressed back against the cool stone wall. Overhead a torch flared into life, illuminating the darkness.

The Master released the wheel and it sprang back round. He scooted in beside them. As the bookcase slid closed Staunch kicked open the Scriptorium door. 'Hey, Master quill scratcher, I've brought your stinking book,' he growled.

Rayne heard something heavy slam onto a desk and Staunch mutter. 'It's time Mali taught him another lesson in obedience.'

The colour drained from the Master's face.

The crab-monster walked past their hiding place and his footsteps faded away.

'What broken Spell turned him into a monster?' said Tom.

'Hopefully a very painful one,' said the Master. 'We must hurry before Mali comes looking. Now Rayne, how do you propose we find the Hall of Spells?'

'The same way I found the secret way up to the Scriptorium.' She turned to face the wall. 'Hello?'

The Master scratched the back of his head. 'The wall told you about the secret way?'

'Sort of.' Rayne tapped the stone. 'Are you still here?'

The wall hissed an answer.

Tom jumped back. 'Oh great. The Grotesques are helping us now.'

'That is by no means certain,' said the Master.

A sharp-tipped horn poked through the stone, followed by a stubby nose and a pair of blinking red eyes. 'What do you want?'

'Do you know the way to the Hall of Spells?'

'Coursse we do. We know where all the roomss are.'

Rayne stepped closer to the wall. 'Will you show us?'

The Grotesque pushed a fat arm through the wall and scratched its horn. 'Maybe. But we already paid you back our favour. Why sshould we help you again?'

Rayne blinked. 'Er . . .'

'Because if you guide us, the Hall of Spells will help us rescue Rayne's mother,' said the Master. 'And once we do, she will owe you a favour.'

Stubby Nose wagged a finger. 'Sshe already owess uss.' Shaking its head, it shrank down into the wall.

'Wait! If you help us, Mam will owe you two favours.'

'Two?' A slow, toothy grin spread across the Grotesque's face. It rolled forwards into the stone and rippled across the wall. Its arms windmilled like it was swimming through water. It stopped and looked back. 'Keep up then.'

'Do you trust the Grotesque to guide us correctly?' asked the Master.

Rayne shrugged. 'I trust it about as much as I trust you.'

A pink tinge stole up the Master's cheeks. 'In that case, you may rely on the creature completely.'

At the end of the passage they reached a small vestibule. A torch ignited, casting a smoky glow over two archways, one leading left and the other leading right. The Grotesque arced upwards across the ceiling and zoomed into the left corridor. Rayne, Tom, and the Master followed. Another torch caught fire up ahead.

Tom glanced back. 'Look.' He pointed to the light from the torches they'd passed. They were slowly extinguishing, returning the corridor to darkness. 'Why are they going out?'

'They have a conservation Spell breathed upon them,' said the Master. 'And a good thing too. If they were left burning, I would spend days replacing them.'

At the end of a long, sloping corridor they skidded to a stop. A wooden door with no handle barred the way.

Stubby Nose poked its head through the wall beside it. 'What are you waiting for?'

'There's no handle,' said Tom.

'You musst go under.'

'Ah, I never thought of that.' The Master crouched down, prised his fingers under the wood and lifted the door like a flap. A smile lit his face. 'The Great Library never ceases to surprise me.' He nodded to Rayne. 'After you.'

Rayne crawled underneath. 'Can I ask a question?'

'Of course, my dear.'

'Why did you and Mam give Mali the Spell of Manipulation?'

They arrived at the top of a flight of steps. The Master ducked his head as he jogged down them. 'That is an old story. Best forgotten,' he murmured.

'Please tell me. Mam never would.'

'Guilt is a hard thing to live with. Sometimes it is easier to pretend a mistake never happened. But you cannot pretend forever. Your mother proved that when she returned to the library two days ago.'

'So she left Penderin to confront her sister?' asked Tom.

The Master nodded. 'She said she was done hiding. Unfortunately, by the time she arrived the

Penderin Spell book was broken and so too were the Spells she carried with her. Mali froze her instantly.'

Cold guilt doused Rayne like a Spell. She slowed her steps.

Reaching the bottom they entered a circular room with six passages leading in different directions. One of the passages was illuminated with firelight. The Master and Tom walked towards it.

Rayne stopped still. 'Why did you give Mali the Spell?'

The Master glanced over his shoulder. Sighing, he turned around. 'Because I was a hot-headed fool. When I discovered the black dictionaries chained in the vault, I was angry. I believed no word should be censored. The Word Masters did not agree so I vowed to set them free. As for your mother, she had been longing to mindwrite pure word-magic and thought this was her chance.'

'I don't believe you. Mam told me copying Spells was safest.'

'I am sure she believes that now. Anyone would believe copying was safer if they had breathed a dark Spell over Mali.'

'So why did she?'

'Mali was skilled in the art of manipulation long before we ever gave her the Spell. She begged us for it. Said it was her chance to help people.' His lips twisted. 'Afterwards we learned our mistake.'

Tom came to stand beside Rayne. 'How?'

'On the day of Meleri's graduation, Mali stole the spark siphon. She planned to freeze your mother and take her spark. When Meleri found out she took her Spell book and fled. Afterwards, all hell broke loose. Mali used her new power to force everyone to smash their books, and you have seen first-hand what that leads to.' He shook his head at the memory. 'It was awful. People were screaming. The Word Masters mutated into horrors.'

A terrible thought lit Rayne's mind. 'My aunt started the monster plague?'

Tom gaped.

The Master plucked at a golden quill embroidered on his robes. 'Started by Mali, yes. But Meleri and I played a part too. And for our mistake we pay a heavy price.'

Rayne stared intently at the Master's face. 'What happened to the Spell Breathers? They couldn't get the plague. Why didn't they do something?'

'Mali swatted them like flies, and then . . .' He bit his lip.

'And then?' urged Rayne.

The Master's hands trembled. His eyes glazed

over and she knew he was no longer seeing her, but something else. 'Mali marched them out into the courtyard. One by one she threw them off the parapet onto the rocks below.' He dropped his voice to a whisper. 'If any survived the fall she held them under the water . . . until they drowned.'

Rayne's knees gave way and she sank to the floor.

'What happened to the other Spell Breathers?' asked Tom. 'The ones who came here after the plague started?'

The Master bowed his head. 'She threw them in the river too.'

The fire torches crackled. Their smoky tendrils curled silently upwards.

A voice echoed along the corridor. 'Why aren't you following me? The Hall of Sspellss iss down here.'

The Master snatched a steadying breath and started towards the Grotesque. Tom followed, ruffling his hair into a wild mess.

Dazed, Rayne stumbled after them. Mali had started the monster plague? And Mam had helped her. She wanted to shout and scream everything was their fault. But she kept quiet, because in her head a small voice whispered, *they weren't in Penderin when you dropped the book.*

Grand wooden doors confronted them, decorated with gold that flickered in the firelight. Submerged in stone beside them, Stubby Nose's red eyes blinked up at Rayne. 'The Hall of Sspellss.'

Tom peered into the dark passage on either side. 'Did we leave the secret way?'

'No,' said the Master. 'The Hall was one of the Word Masters' best-kept secrets. They would not risk anyone stumbling across it.'

'I have done asss you wisshed.' Stubby Nose sank into the stone. 'Be ssure to tell your mother.'

'Hey, you can't leave now,' said Tom. 'You have to show us the way back.'

Stubby Nose reappeared. 'That wass not part of our bargain.'

Tom sighed and said, 'Will you show us if *I* owe you a favour?'

The Grotesque grinned wickedly. Lifting fat arms behind its head it lay back in the stone. Its belly poked up as it floated against the wall.

'You will not join us?' asked the Master.

'What'ss it worth?'

The Master cocked an eyebrow at Tom and Rayne. 'Never mind. I think we will save our favours.' He grasped the door handle and swung it wide.

Cold darkness and a cacophony of clinks and tinks washed over them.

A flare of flames lit a lofty hall. Its vaulted ceiling was hung with a golden candelabrum. Below the candles, packed tightly together, stood four columns of tall wooden shelves, each laden with blue glass bottles.

The Master stepped inside and blew out his cheeks. 'An ocean of crystal. I never dreamed there would be so many. Far more than any Spell book.'

Rayne's hand stole across the pit of her stomach. With her spark gone she couldn't feel the tingle of word-magic. She would have been delighted two days ago. Now, she felt numb.

Tom inspected the nearest shelf. 'That tinking noise. It's coming from the bottles.'

Rayne stepped beside him. 'It's like they're tapping on the glass. Asking to be let out.'

Every bottle was the same size. Wooden stoppers, shaped like quills, were wedged into their stubby necks. Circled around each was a length of string and a label. Peering inside a bottle, Rayne saw dark, inky words writhe and bounce against the glass.

Tom flipped over a label. 'The Spell of Disappearing.' He grinned. 'Do you think that's the same as the Spell of Invisibility Frank told us about?'

'Hardly,' said the Master. 'A disappearing Spell is deadly. People who disappear never return.'

'Could be just what we need for Mali, then.' Tom gripped the bottle, then cried out as the glass shattered, slicing into his fingers.

For a heartbeat, the word-magic twisted and spun in the air, then dropped into his skin. Tom shot a helpless look at Rayne and vanished.

THE HALL OF SPELLS

Rayne lunged forwards. 'Tom!' Her arms swiped uselessly through air, falling by her side. She swung round to the Master. 'Quick, find a Spell to bring him back!'

'I . . . I do not know of such a Spell,' said the Master, gaping at the space where Tom had been standing.

Rayne's hand flitted across the bottles. They clinked ominously as she hurriedly read their labels. 'No, no, no! Tom's always hated Spells. He can't disappear. He'll never stop going on about it.'

The Master shook his head. 'I should have thought of this. The Spells have been down here for centuries. All that tapping has made the glass brittle.'

The bottles wobbled as Rayne stepped along the shelf, crouching to read their labels then springing on tiptoes to read more.

Gently, the Master stilled her arm. 'My dear, stop. There is nothing we can do.'

She turned, tears brimming. 'I can't stop. Tom never would.'

'We have no choice. We cannot bring back someone who does not exist.'

His words crashed over her like a bucket of ice.

A movement pulsed in the corner of her eye. For a second Rayne saw a shape.

She stared at the empty space.

The shape flickered and vanished, but not before her eyes locked on a strand of blond hair. Slowly, she reached out. When the shape flickered again her fingers squashed into something warm and soft and boy-shaped. 'Tom?'

Very faint and far away, she heard the cry of her name.

Rayne gripped Tom's shoulder and his body flickered and fluttered like a butterfly.

The Master's mouth fell open.

Tom shuddered back to existence, as solid as a brick wall. 'What happened?' he panted.

'Word-magic. It made you disappear.' Rayne

beamed a huge smile. 'But then you came back.'

The Master shook Tom's elbow. 'Next time, please consult a dictionary before you douse yourself in word-magic for which you do not know the precise meaning!' He put on his spectacles and peered at Tom. 'How do you feel?'

'My skin is tingling.' Tom patted his arms and chest, staining his tunic red from the cut on his fingers. 'I thought you said people who disappear never come back?'

The Master straightened up. 'Generally they do not. I can think of only one explanation. These Spells are so ancient their word-magic is now stale.'

'Stale?' Tom gave a shaky laugh. 'Lucky me.'

Rayne frowned. 'You mean we can't use these Spells to get my spark back?'

'Tom's Spell worked for a moment. That is all we need . . . if we choose wisely.'

Rayne walked into the aisle and gazed at the myriad of blue. 'But how do we choose? It will take forever to read every label.'

'And Staunch is even now pouring my many faults into Mali's ears.' The Master scanned the shelves. 'The Word Masters will have catalogued these Spells somehow.'

Rayne pointed to the end of the shelf. 'This row

is marked with the letter D.'

'Good. That tells us they are stored in alphabetical order. Let us begin our search by choosing a letter.'

Rayne turned on her heel.

'Where are you going?' called Tom.

'S for Spark!'

She jogged between the rows until she reached one marked with the letter S. Turning the corner she skidded to a stop and groaned. The shelves here were taller than the ones by the door. Hundreds of blue bottles gleamed in the candlelight.

The Master passed her, striding to the middle of the shelves. 'Next we find Spells beginning SP. If there is a Spell for spark removal we should find it quickly.' He started turning labels. 'And for goodness' sake, please be careful with the bottles.'

Tom crouched to inspect the lower shelves. 'There's one thing about Mali I don't understand.'

The Master inched along the shelf. 'Only one thing? I find every aspect of her puzzling.'

'If Mali's so desperate to get hold of a spark, why didn't she take it from her sister two days ago?'

Rayne grimaced. 'She prefers mine because it's *fresher.*'

'Ugh,' Tom made a face. 'So why didn't she take

your mam's and chuck it away?'

'She should have, of course,' said the Master. 'But Mali is mad for revenge. Leaving Meleri her spark allows her a shred of hope. When she realizes she is unable to use it, that hope will fester. Just like when she learns Rayne gave away her spark, that will hurt her like a knife in the gut.'

Rayne dug her teeth into her lip and concentrated on the labels.

The Master straightened up and began smoothing his beard. 'You are right, Tom. Mali has made a mistake. Perhaps we can trick her into making another.'

Rayne turned a label. A jolt of excitement shot through her. 'Listen . . .'

༄ THE SPELL OF SPARK CLEANSING ༄

Scour and evict
Rid and strip
Hollow out smooth
Detach and remove
Spark, fly free
Come to me!

'It's perfect,' she said, her eyes shining.

Tom stood up. 'If it works.' He read the labels of

the bottles nearby. 'There's only one bottle with that label.'

Gently she lifted the bottle and cradled it in her hands. The Spell tapped against the glass, trying to get out.

Tom looked from the Rayne to the Master. 'So, what's your idea? Walk up to Mali and ask her to stand still while we pour word-magic over her?'

'Something like that.' The Master touched the black Spell folder in his belt. 'First, I will allay her suspicions by giving her what she wants.'

Rayne shook her head. 'There has to be another way.'

'Do not worry, your mother is not with Mali. By the time she comes to mindwrite the torment Spell she will no longer have your spark.'

'How will we get it out of her?' asked Tom.

'Rayne, you must plead with Mali to see your mother. Tell her you want your mother's forgiveness. She will be unable to resist. And while she is distracted we will slip her the spark Spell.'

Rayne nodded. 'And my spark will fly to me.'

Tom rolled his eyes. 'This is a rubbish plan. What if the Spell doesn't work? Or Mali sees what you're up to and freezes us all?'

Rayne eased the bottle into her tunic pocket and

held it there. 'Do you have a better idea?'

Tom ruffled his hair. 'What if I take a Spell too?'

'Unwise,' said the Master. 'The more we take, the higher the risk we get hurt. You may not be so lucky next time.'

'Not if we take something harmless. Something like . . .' Tom crouched and pointed to a bottle on the lower shelf. 'The Spell of Sleep. If the glass breaks, the worst that happens is I fall asleep. I could wait outside Mali's study. If something goes wrong, I can run in and throw the Spell at her.'

Rayne's eyebrows shot up. 'Tom, are you all right? You're acting as if you like word-magic.'

The Master grinned. 'I think that Spell has changed him.'

Tom hunched a shoulder. 'Maybe we do need some Spells after all.' He glanced up at Rayne and winked. 'Don't tell your mam.'

☙ ❧

The rising passage ended abruptly beside a wall. Stubby Nose pushed through the centre. 'Mali'ss sstudy liess beyond. Pussh my sstone to open the wall.'

The Master nodded. 'Well then . . . Rayne? Tom? Shall we?'

Rayne chewed her lip. Last time she'd had a plan

Mam's Spell book had fallen on the fire. Tom was right. This was a rubbish plan.

The Master touched the wall.

'What if I mess up again,' Rayne blurted.

'You will not,' said the Master.

'You don't know that.'

'Look, we've all messed up,' said Tom. 'You with the book, me with the tunnel,' he looked at the Master. 'And you too. But—'

'So why will this time be any different?'

'Because we were on our own then. This time we'll be together.' He held out his hand, palm down. 'Deal?'

Rayne stared at his hand, wanting more than anything to believe him. Hadn't Mam made a mistake too? And she'd never stopped trying to put it right.

She grasped his hand.

A ghost of a smile lit the Master's eyes and he sandwiched their hands between his own. 'Deal.'

Tom looked at the Grotesque. 'What about you?'

Stubby Nose blew a raspberry and sank into the stone.

The Master squeezed their hands. 'The only deals it likes are ones with favours attached.' His smile faded. 'Rayne, give me the bottle. It should be me who pours it over Mali.'

She shook her head firmly. 'She tricked me into giving my spark away. It's my turn now.'

'Are you sure? You can no longer direct word-magic with your breath. You must be careful none of the Spell splashes on you.'

'What does that matter? I don't have a spark.'

'If you get splashed, you may never have a spark again.'

'Oh.' Rayne pressed her lips together. 'Better my spark lives in no one than inside her.'

'As you wish.' Solemnly, the Master pulled the folder from his belt and pushed his fingers into the wall.

The wall scraped to the side. Rayne peered out. They were back in the vaults. To the left, the portcullis gaped open, revealing the hulking shadows of the black bookcases. Across the way, Mali's study door was ajar. Her voice rose to greet them.

'Enough moaning, Staunch. I told you to stay with him. Perhaps I should teach you a lesson in obedience.'

The Master put a finger to his lips and they crept forward. Tom crouched by the wall cradling his blue bottle. He nodded to them.

Wiping the back of his hand across his mouth, the Master stepped inside.

'Where've you been hiding?' demanded Mali. 'You'd better have my Spell, or I swear you'll feel my hand.'

'Mistress, forgive my delay.' The Master bowed his head. 'I have it here.'

Heart pounding, Rayne walked in beside him and hovered by the door.

Mali beamed. 'You've brought my naive niece. How thoughtful.'

'She has come to beg a favour,' said the Master.

Mali chuckled as she drew Mam's red cloak tightly around herself. 'Save your breath, you're never getting it back.'

Rayne fought down a rush of anger. 'Please. I want to see Mam. I want to say sorry.'

A speck of wall rippled behind Mali's head. Stubby Nose pushed through and waved its arms wildly.

'Oooh, what a good idea,' purred Mali. 'Yes, tell my sister how you thought so little of her gift, you couldn't wait to give it to me.' Mali walked around the desk, grasped the tapestry map and yanked it aside. 'But then, I think she already knows.'

Rayne's heart jumped and then dropped like a stone. In the dark recess behind the tapestry stood Mam, her eyes fixed in an unblinking stare. Her arms clamped rigid to her sides. She was frozen to the spot.

TIME TO SHINE

The Master gasped. 'Meleri's here?'

'After our years apart, I like to keep her close at hand,' mocked Mali.

Rayne tore her eyes from Mam to stare at the black folder, trembling in the Master's grip. She had to get Mam away. Now.

She dashed towards the alcove. Mali flicked her fingers and Rayne hurtled backwards. She smacked into the wall and slumped beside the bench. 'Let Mam go,' she croaked.

Staunch's fingers dug into her shoulder and she jerked to her feet. His massive pincer snapped open. 'Shall I slice her, mistress?'

Mali laughed. 'Free her, so she can enjoy our

touching family reunion.'

Staunch released her. Desperate to help Mam, Rayne stayed where she was. She couldn't pour the spark Spell if Mali froze her again.

'Come on then. Let's have your sorry.' Mali tapped her foot.

Rayne looked at Mam's lifeless face. 'Oh, Mam. I'm sorry!'

Mali sneered. 'Pathetic.' She turned to the Master. 'Don't stand there gawping. Hand over the Spell.'

The Master hesitated.

Mali clicked her fingers and he jerked to attention. He marched to the desk and slapped down the folder. Mali poked him in the side. 'And you will stay like that until you learn to do what you're told.'

Rayne edged closer. Time was running out. She had to get her spark before Mali could mindwrite the Spell and breathe it over Mam.

Mali opened the folder and read the torment Spell. She wriggled with delight. 'Excellent. I can't wait to gift this to my sister.' She snapped her fingers. Mam's long braids flew back, and she toppled to the floor like a skittle.

Mali chuckled. 'Oops.'

Staunch clicked his pincer appreciatively. It sounded like clapping.

The bottle Rayne held inside her pocket trembled.

Mali bent over Mam. 'Do you have any final words, sister?' She beckoned Staunch to her side. For a second their backs were to Rayne.

Sliding the bottle from her pocket, she twisted the stopper, then bit her lip. It was stuck.

Staunch slid a hand under Mam's shoulder and rolled her onto her back. Blood trickled from her nose.

Past caring whether the glass broke, Rayne gripped the bottle and yanked the stopper. It jerked free. Quick as lightning she straightened her arm and tipped the Spell. Words gushed out, twisting and writhing into Mali's back.

Mali shivered. Her head snapped up.

Rayne whipped the bottle behind her back. A few inky words splashed into her skirt and boots. Staring innocently at Mali, she fiddled the stopper home.

Arching an eyebrow, Mali stood and flicked her fingers. Mam's stiff body relaxed. Grimacing, she slowly pushed herself up onto her knees. Staunch hauled her upright and marched her to the bench.

Rayne slipped the bottle back into her pocket, her eyes glued to Mali's stomach, waiting for her golden spark to emerge.

Mali walked back around her desk and studied the folder.

Rayne frowned. Spells were supposed to work instantly. Even if it was stale, Tom had vanished in seconds. She stared at the ink stain on her skirt and boot. Had Mali got enough?

Mam smeared blood across her cheek as she wiped her nose. 'Well, sister . . . all these years . . . all this suffering. Are you happy now?' She bent her head to one side. 'You don't look happy.'

Mali glared at her. 'Once I've dealt with you, I will be ecstatic.'

Mam looked at Rayne and her eyes glowed. She held out her hand. 'Are you all right, love? I've been worried about you.'

Rayne clasped Mam's hand and sank to her knees. 'I'm sorry, Mam. Sorry for everything.'

'Don't be. I am sorry.' Mam kissed her head. 'I should have told you everything years ago.'

'We have to get you away. Mali wants to breathe the Spell of Torment over you!'

Mam's eyes flew to the Master, still frozen beside the desk. Her lip curled. 'What's he done now?'

Rayne squeezed Mam's hand, wanting to tell her he was on their side, but she daren't risk it.

'The same for me as he once did for you.' Mali sneered.

'Then he is a bigger fool than I thought.'

'Falling over has knocked you senseless, sister. I can remember a time you couldn't wait to mindwrite a Spell from the black dictionaries.'

'And for that I blame myself every day,' said Mam, bitterly. 'I should never have believed your lies. You don't have it in you to help anyone.'

Mali's eyes glittered. 'Don't worry. You'll have other things on your mind shortly.'

Rayne's eyes slid to the folder on the desk. She had to rip the Spell before Mali finished memorizing the rhyme. Releasing Mam's hand, she edged towards the desk.

Staunch's pincer tapped her shoulder. 'Close enough, girlie,' he growled.

Mali read the folder again. A smirk played about her lips. 'Well sister, after years watching you dribble words from your head, it's finally my turn.' She opened a drawer and brought out a blank parchment.

A bead of sweat trickled down Rayne's back. Her eyes raked over Mali, desperate for her spark to emerge.

Mam stood, stepping towards her sister. 'Please. Let Rayne go.'

'Oh no.' Mali smirked. 'Your daughter and her spark will stay with me.'

Mam's face crumpled. 'What's wrong with you?

I gave you everything you asked for. But that was never good enough for you, was it?'

'You didn't give me your spark,' spat Mali.

'I loved you!'

'Love? What good is love?' She read the folder again, then pushed it aside. Her eyes locked on Mam. Her lips soundlessly chanting the Spell. All at once her face darkened, as if a shadow blocked the candlelight.

Rayne twisted her fingers together as brown, sludgy words seeped from Mali's forehead and splattered onto the parchment. They shuffled around each other, forming themselves into the rhyme.

Mam's face tinged green, and for a heartbeat Rayne was glad she had no spark to feel the horror of the Spell.

Mali picked up the parchment and checked its spelling against the file. Satisfied, she stalked around her desk. 'Say goodbye to your sanity, sister.'

Taking a deep breath, she blew the Spell straight at Mam. It roared towards her like a storm cloud.

'*No!*' Rayne screamed.

A golden glow lit Mali's stomach. Too late, the spark was breaking free.

Mam pursed her lips and blew Mali's Spell off course. Confused, the word-magic slowed, rolling and crashing on itself like a wave.

Tom banged open the study door and rushed inside, holding his blue bottle aloft. He stopped, looking from Mam to Mali and back again. 'Which one's your mam?'

Ignoring him, Mali tried to blow the words back at Mam, but the spark hurtled out of her, leaving her powerless. Rayne shot up a hand and caught its pulsing warmth. Instantly, bile rose in her throat as the echo of dark word-magic tingled over her.

The words careered sideways and sank into a shelf of books. Where they touched, the pages oozed yellow slime.

'How?' Mali howled. 'I smashed the siphon!'

Triumphantly, Rayne lifted the blue bottle from her pocket.

Mali ground her teeth and crooked her fingers.

'Don't touch her!' Mam launched herself at Mali, twisting her arm back. They grappled across the desk, knocking the Master to the floor.

In the struggle, the red cloak slipped from Mali's shoulders. Rayne blinked. Apart from their hair they looked identical. But inside they were as different as night and day.

Staunch levelled his pincer at Rayne. 'Give back the spark, or I will rip it from you.'

Tom's frown cleared. He smashed the bottle into Staunch's claw and jumped back. Writhing words sank into the pincer. Staunch gave a startled grunt and his eyelids fluttered. His knees buckled, and he toppled forwards. As he fell, Mam shoved a snarling Mali underneath him. His deadweight crashed against her shoulder, pinning her left arm and hand to the floor. She tried to roll away, but the giant's body held her firm.

The Master shuddered and got to his feet. He turned his head to Mali and smiled grimly. 'See how you like being stuck for a while.'

'Traitor!' she shrieked, trying to wriggle free. 'I'll freeze Grotesques to your entire body until you beg for mercy!'

Slipping the belt from his robe he wound it around Mali's mouth. She tried to bite him. 'Possibly,' he said. 'But until then, we will no hear more of you.'

Mam plucked the folder off the desk and ripped the Master's Spell to shreds. The pieces fell like confetti.

Rayne gazed at the brilliant light shining between the cracks in her fingers. Holding her spark felt like coming home. She drank it down, enjoying the taste of warm honey. A golden glow shone out of her middle. For a heart-stopping moment she thought the spark would fly out. But the glow subsided, and she sighed with relief.

Mam picked up her red cloak and knelt before Rayne. 'Real torment was hearing you give your spark away.' She spread the cloak around her daughter and secured the clasp. 'I am proud of you for taking it back. Never forget who you are.'

It felt like the Spell of Gladness. Mam was safe, and her insides felt full, like she'd feasted on all her favourite foods at once. 'I won't lose it again. I promise.'

Mam folded her into a tight hug and kissed her cheek. Slowly, she got to her feet and turned to the Master. 'It seems I should thank you.'

He bowed his head. 'You are welcome.'

Staunch's snores echoed about the room.

Mam looked at the blue glass lying on the floor. 'I see you found the Hall of Spells.' She arched an eyebrow at Tom. 'Changed your mind about Spells, have you?'

Tom blushed. 'So, what do we do now?'

The Master walked calmly to the door and pulled the key from the lock. 'Now? Now we run for it!'

SHE WHO FIGHTS
AND RUNS AWAY

Mam hurried Rayne out of the study. Tom scooted behind. The Master banged the door, turned the lock, and threw the key into the secret way. 'That should hold them for a while.'

'If Staunch wakes up, won't he just kick it open?' said Tom.

'Ah.' The Master scratched his head. 'Probably.'

'How long before he wakes?' asked Rayne.

'That depends on the Spell, and Staunch is very strong of course. He could sleep for a minute or a day.'

'I hope it's forever,' Rayne muttered.

Mam touched the master's arm. 'Will you help me repair my book?'

He nodded. 'I have already promised to do so. Your book is waiting for us in the Scriptorium, along with your bottle of ink.'

Mam heaved a sigh. 'We must take them to a safe place. If she doesn't know where we are, she can't bring us back with that dammed hand of hers.'

The Master walked towards the portcullis. 'The vault's secret way will be the quickest route up.'

Mam nodded. 'Yes, I remember.' She and Tom followed the Master inside. Rayne trailed behind. Going through the vault was the quickest way, but the rotting dictionaries made her feel queasy.

'I hate this place.' Mam shivered. 'Last time we were here we did a terrible thing. These words are evil.'

'No word is evil, Meleri. But in the wrong hands they can be horribly twisted.'

Mam gave the Master a look that said, let's not discuss that again.

Rayne walked quickly to the back wall and pushed the bottom stone to open the secret way.

Mam peered inside. 'How did you know which stone to press?'

'A Grotesque showed me.'

'A Grotesque?' Mam followed Rayne up the steps. 'From the Grotesquery?'

'No . . . from your Spell book.'

Tom and the Master stepped through the wall and it scraped shut. They climbed up the spiral in pitch black. It seemed making a confession easier. 'Don't be angry, Mam. I helped them escape the mud.' She explained how she'd dropped the book on the fire and how she'd returned the Grotesques home.

'I'm not angry, love. I'm glad you did. I took them to protect my book from Mali. But it was a mistake. It made you frightened of the book, and I hurt the Grotesques, terribly.' She was silent for a minute, then said, 'So you helped them and now they're helping you?'

'Not exactly,' said Rayne.

'They're helping in return for favours,' said Tom.

'Yes, and . . . um we sort of promised you'd owe them a favour.'

'Two favourss,' hissed the wall.

Mam stopped climbing. 'Oh . . . I suppose it's only fair.'

'Oomph.' Tom barged into Mam's back. 'Sorry. Why aren't there any torches in here?'

'No use for them,' said the Master. 'When the dictionaries were chained in the vault, no one had any intention of going back.'

'There's light up ahead,' said Rayne.

The sound of tinkling glass brought a shaft of rainbow light. One by one they stepped into the Scriptorium and trooped down the row of desks to Mam's satchel lying at the end. Quickly, she unstrapped its buckles and brought out her book. She stared at the cherry wood cover. 'Hello, old friend.' Her eyes filled with tears and she hugged it close. 'Did you see our friends change?'

Rayne clasped her hands. 'Old Flo, the blacksmith, the warden.' Her voice dropped to a whisper. 'Jenna . . . Little Jack . . .'

'The scouts too,' said Tom.

'Oh Mam, they'd all be safe if I hadn't dropped your book!'

'Hush.' She held her bottle of golden ink to the light. 'See, we can still make everyone better. You two did a brave thing coming to the Great Library. How did you know to come here?'

'The Spell of Finding was at the bottom of your satchel. It summoned a fox to help us. Or I thought it did. Turns out it was helping Mali instead.'

'A fox you say? Where's it now?'

'Somewhere you will never see again,' said the Master, holding the satchel open. Mam stored the book inside.

'The fox wasn't all bad,' said Rayne. 'If he hadn't brought us here we wouldn't be together now.'

'Fox or no fox, after you dropped my book it looks to me like you've taken good care of it. Taking responsibility for the villagers, like a proper Spell Breather.'

Rayne smiled.

Tom plucked a quill from the desk and started fiddling with it. 'I dug a tunnel under the barrier,' he blurted.

Mam pursed her lips. 'So that's how Penderin appeared on the living maps. Oh, Tom.'

'Sorry,' said Tom, going red. 'I know now it was a stupid thing to do. When we get home I'll fill it in.'

'Please do. Even though Mali knows where the village is now, she won't be able to touch us if the barrier is intact. When everyone is better, I will come out and she and I will finish what we started.'

'I will help you, Mam.'

Mam frowned. 'No, this is not your responsibility.'

'Please don't keep secrets again. I want to help, and you said yourself everything would be better if you'd talked to me.' She put her hand over Mam's. 'We won't make mistakes if we work together.'

Mam's frown melted. 'Goodness, you have

become very wise in the last two days.' She nodded. 'We'll talk it all over when we get home.'

The Master slid open a panel in the wall and brought out two parchments, both scripted with Spells.

'Those words aren't from the black dictionaries, are they?' asked Mam.

The Master lifted his chin. 'Some of them. The first is the Spell of Immobility. We can use it to beat Mali at her own game.'

Mam sighed. 'And what's the other?'

'The Spell of Apnoea.'

'Appy-what?' asked Tom.

'Apnoea. It means temporary holding of breath. Very useful if you are under water.' The Master swallowed. 'I wrote it after Mali . . . after she pushed everyone over the parapet.' He looked at Mam. 'I came to Penderin to ask you to breathe the Spell over us.'

'Why?'

A pained looked came into his eyes. 'To prevent her doing to us what she did to them.'

Mam took the Spell and nodded. 'If the Great Library ever re-opens, we will make sure everyone knows about this Spell.'

The Master sat down, opened Mam's bottle of ink and dipped a quill inside. 'If I write the immobility

Spell in your ink, you can breathe it straight from the sheet without copying.' His quill scratched across a parchment.

'But then I'll only be able to use it once,' said Mam.

'If you land it on her, once is all we need.' The Master dusted the sheet with sand and handed the golden Spell to Mam. Her brow creased, and her head bent slowly to read the parchment.

'What's wrong, Mam?'

'The Spell feels slow and heavy.' Her lips twitched. 'It's what you would call a weird one.'

The ink bottles lining the entrance to the secret way rattled. Startled, they turned to stare at the hidden door.

'Uh-oh,' said Tom.

'We have to go,' said the Master. 'But first we must collect the Master Book from the Dictionary Room.' He packed everything into the satchel, buckled the straps and put it across his shoulder. 'We can make the breath-holding Spell when we are in the secret way.'

They hurried into the corridor and strode towards the grand staircase in the main hall. Rounding the gilt bannister they stopped dead. Staunch stood on the first step, barring the way. His massive claw scissored as he held it aloft. He pointed towards the grand entrance doors. 'You're wanted outside,' he growled, advancing towards them.

'Let us not be hasty,' said the Master. 'Let us go and I promise to find the broken Spell that turned you into a monster and repair it for you.'

Staunch sneered. 'I prefer being this way. I was weak before.' He shoved his claw under the Master's chin. The pincer sliced open. 'Strong is better.'

They stumbled outside onto the terrace. At the bottom of the sweeping steps, hands on hips, Mali waited for them. 'I knew you wouldn't leave without the Master Book,' she jeered. 'You know your problem, sister? You're always too eager to help people.'

'Helping people is the best feeling in the world. You would know that if you'd ever tried,' said Mam. 'Do something kind for once and let us go.'

'The torment Spell will seem a kindness compared to what I will do to you now.'

Mam struggled to lift the immobility Spell. Her hands shook as she raised it to her face.

'I'll help,' said Rayne, touching a corner of the parchment. She tried to step closer to Mam, but it was like walking in treacle.

'How pathetic.' Mali crooked her freezing fingers at them. 'Even the two of you are no match for me.'

Mam's arm circled Rayne's waist, pulling her close. Rayne read the Spell and understood at once why she felt so sluggish.

ᏩᎦ THE SPELL OF IMMOBILITY ᎤᎧ

Static and still
Suspension of will
Stationary and passive
Disabled, stopped, inactive
Dormant heavy bone
Anchored solid stone

Together they blew the Spell free.

Writhing word-magic blazed straight at Mali. She sprang aside.

Mam twisted her lips and the words swung back on target.

Mali fled to the dead trees at the centre of the courtyard. The words scudded behind, gaining ground. She slid behind a trunk and the words sank into the bark. A few letters nicked Mali's hand, sinking into her little finger.

Howling, she shrugged her shoulder, trying to make her arm move, but it hung limply by her side. She stepped around the tree and pointed her other hand at Mam. 'My turn,' she snarled.

'The wrong hand!' cried Tom.

Rayne's feet lifted off the ground and she shot upwards. Mam, Tom, and the Master tumbled through the air beside her.

Laughing, Mali ran through the courtyard, her right arm swinging uselessly by her side. They glided behind, as if pulled along on an invisible string. When she reached the parapet wall, Mali whipped her hand down.

Rayne dropped like a stone. Her hands and knees scraped the cobbles as she skidded along the ground, thudding against the wall. When she looked up her blood ran cold. Mam, Tom, and the Master teetered on top of the parapet. Below them, the sheer vertical drop over jagged rocks, down to the river.

Mali snapped her fingers and her prisoners spun to face her. Only their legs were frozen now, their arms flailed as they swayed backwards.

'If you throw me off, you will have no one to write your Spells,' said the Master.

'What use are you to me, without a spark? Tell me where I can find the Hall of Spells and I will consider not dashing your brains on the rocks.'

Finding her balance, Mam crossed her arms. 'We believed your lies once. Never again.'

A grinning Staunch came to stand next to Mali. 'Persuade the boy to tell you what I want to know,' she commanded.

Leering, the monster advanced on Tom.

'I knew I should have picked up another Spell bottle,' he muttered.

'Wait.' Rayne got to her feet, cold wind whipping hair across her face.

Mali's eyes glittered dangerously. 'Would you like to see how I deal with Spell Breathers?'

'Let them go and I will show you how to find the Hall of Spells,' Rayne lied.

'Oh, you'll do that anyway. But first you will watch me push them off, watch their bodies bounce on the rocks . . . and watch me hold them under the water.'

'Let the children go,' begged Mam. 'Our fight has nothing to do with them.'

'No! The boy dies, and after Staunch rips out your girl's spark, I will toss her over to join you.' Mali laughed. 'Then I will be a Spell Breather once more. This time, I will be the *last* Spell Breather!'

ALL YOU NEED IS . . .

Mali flicked her fingers. The Master collapsed off the wall and rolled on the cobbles. 'I have need of your services after all,' she said. 'Once you have paid for your treachery, of course.'

Rayne crouched beside him. The bruise on his forehead was now an angry graze.

'There must be *something* we can do,' muttered Tom.

'Yes, but what?' said Rayne. 'We've no Spells, and besides she'd throw you off before Mam finished mindwriting any.'

She wracked her brain. She was a Spell Breather, Mali wasn't. There must be something she could do. She thought back to Mali, mindwriting the torment

Spell with pure word-magic. Her spark had done that. It was back inside her. Could she do the same? She groaned. Even if she knew how, there was no time. Mali would freeze her long before she finished.

She looked longingly at Mam. The cold wind swept up the rock face, making her braids dance. Mam looked back with sad eyes, like this was all her fault, like she'd let everyone down. But it wasn't true. Mam looked after everyone, she never let anyone down.

The Master rose unsteadily to his feet. 'I promise you, Mali, if you throw them off, I will never write you another Spell. I do not care what you do to me.'

Mali cocked an eye at Staunch.

'Stay very still, little man,' he growled, opening his pincer. He slid his claw around the Master's neck. A streak of red glistened on his skin.

Rayne squeezed her eyes shut and tried to think of a simple Spell. Her mind was blank. She wanted Mam. Longed to be home. Safe, just like they'd always been. She remembered Mam's last words the night she left Penderin. *'Always remember, I love you. First, last and everywhere in between.'*

The word love beat in her brain; it chimed with her beating heart.

Mali stalked towards Mam on the wall, tilting

her head. 'This is the last time I will ever look up to you, sister. You have nothing I want now.' She flung her hand above her head.

'Please, no,' Rayne croaked.

Love rolled across her like a wave. It surged and swelled until her head tingled with it.

Bright lights glowed around her face. She heard Tom gasp.

They shone brighter and she had to squint through the haze to see Mam.

She blinked. Suspended in front of her face were four golden letters, gleaming in the sunlight.

L.O.V.E.

Her heart leapt at the wonder of them. Her first Spell. And it was pure word-magic.

Mam's face lit with a smile. The Spell's shimmer reflected in her eyes as tears slipped down her cheeks. 'Spell Breather,' she whispered.

Mali glanced over her shoulder and began to giggle. 'Pathetic! It will take more than love to save your mother.'

Mam's foot jerked into the air and she leaned backwards.

'You're wrong,' said Rayne.

She blew her love to Mam. Its shining letters wafted towards the wall.

Staunch grunted. Out of the corner of her eye Rayne saw the Master shrink. His robes collapsed, and the satchel bumped to the ground. His red head slipped through Staunch's claw and he dropped to the cobbles in a squirming mass of fur.

Rayne's eyes stretched wide. *'Frank?'*

The long body of a fox slithered free of the robes and scampered towards Mali. He leapt into the air, pushing her into the path of the Spell.

L.O.V.E. sank into her chest. In stunned silence, she gaped at them, then tipped back her head and screamed.

Released from Mali's hold, Mam lost her balance and fell backwards.

Rayne lunged across the wall, wrapping her arms about Mam's waist. Tom grabbed Mam's outstretched arms and together they bundled her down onto the cobbles, collapsing in a heap on the ground.

Mali sank to her knees and crawled beside them. She raked her fingers down Mam's sleeve. 'Sister! What have I done? I nearly killed you. Tell me you're all right,' she begged. 'I'm sorry. *Forgive me!'*

'Get off.' Mam pushed Mali away and got to her feet. She pulled Rayne into her arms. 'I love you too, sweetheart.'

Rayne hugged Mam tight. 'I tried to mindwrite a word to save you.'

'You did,' said Mam staring in wonder at Mali, on her knees, sobbing. 'I think you saved all of us.'

Frank pattered up to them and sighed. 'Love. It is the strongest, truest, sweetest word in the whole of the Great Library. No other Spell could have bettered it.'

Tom stared at Rayne. 'I thought you said you couldn't mindwrite?'

Rayne prodded her forehead. 'I didn't think I could.' She looked down at Frank. 'You're the Word Master? You've been with us the whole time?'

His amber eyes gazed solemnly up at her. 'I am sorry for deceiving you. Can you forgive me?'

Her mouth twitched up at the corner. 'I will if you repair Mam's Spell book.'

'Then I shall do so at once.' He padded towards his robes, nosed under the hem and wriggled inside. Instantly the cloth ballooned into the shape of a man and the Master stood before them once more.

Not the Master, thought Rayne. Frank.

Staunch pointed his claw at Rayne. 'What have you done to my mistress? You've bewitched her.' He snatched the satchel from the ground and ran to the wall. 'Change her back, or I will throw your Spell book in the river.'

Mam stretched out her arm. 'No!'

'Give that back, you fool.' Frank launched himself at the crab-monster.

They grappled. Frank's two hands clasped around the giant claw, trying to push it away from his face. Staunch, easily stronger, pushed Frank flat across the wall. 'If you want this satchel, little man, then you can go over with it.'

'Watch out!' shouted Tom.

Staunch shoved hard and lost his footing. He rolled across Frank's body and they toppled sideways, falling onto the rocks below.

Mam rushed to the wall. '*My book!*'

The satchel bounced as it rolled down the slope and splashed into the river.

Rayne clutched Tom's shoulder. They leaned over the parapet, watching Frank and Staunch plummet down the rock face. 'We have to help him!'

The struggling pair plunged into the water. White foam rippled outwards.

'He'll be all right,' said Rayne, breathing hard, glancing at Mali. She was huddled beside the wall crying, oblivious to what had happened. 'She won't hold him under. And he's got his bones this time, he can swim.'

The foam dissipated.

Tom sagged against the wall. 'Come on, Frank. Swim!'

The water stilled.

Mam pulled them back from the edge. 'He's gone.'

'He can't be.' Rayne strained to break free. '*Frank!*'

'Hush, love.' Mam folded her into a hug, tears rolling down her cheeks. 'There's nothing we can do for him now. There's nothing we can do for any of them . . .'

⁙

Sunshine slanted through the trees as they sat on a bench in the courtyard. Mam and Mali sat side by side. 'I won't ask you to forgive me,' said Mali. 'How could you? I will never forgive myself.'

'If Mother were here, she would forgive you,' said Mam quietly. 'Maybe in time . . .'

Mali brushed her wet eyes. 'What will you do now?'

'Go home to Penderin. With the Spell book gone I can't heal them. But I can still help them.'

Rayne's heart sank to her boots. Mam was safe, but not their friends. And now they never would be.

Mam turned to Mali. 'Come with us?'

Mali's smile was lopsided. 'I don't think I'd be very welcome, do you?' She squeezed Mam's hand. 'I will stay here and try to mend the broken Spell books. After what I did, their Spell Breathers never will.'

Mam raised Mali's right hand and let it go. It flopped by her side. 'You cannot repair anything with one hand.'

'Like you, I have to try. And who knows, I might find Frank?'

Mam bit her bottom lip. 'I could breathe a Spell over your arm?'

'Don't you dare,' said Mali. 'This arm will be my penance. A remembrance for the hurt I've caused. Especially to you and my niece.' She turned to Rayne. 'I am truly sorry.'

Rayne opened her mouth, then closed it, not knowing what to say.

Mam stood. 'Well . . . we'd best get going.'

'How will you get home?' asked Mali.

'We have a boat moored by the quay,' said Tom.

Mali lifted her left hand. 'I could send you home. It will be quicker.'

Rayne and Tom exchanged worried looks.

Mam shook her head. 'No, sister,' she said firmly. 'Besides, we must stop at the Grotesquery. I have an apology to make.'

The Grotesquery hissed.

Head bowed, Mam stood before its whirling mass of teeth and horns. 'I am sorry I hurt you,' she said. 'What I did was wrong.'

'Sstill running away?' mocked the Grotesquery.

'The time for running is over. I could have slipped out via the secret way. Instead I chose to come here.'

Stubby Nose poked its head through the wall. Its red eyes raked over her. 'What about our favourss? You and the boy owe uss.'

Mam stepped closer. 'When you need me, send word and I will come and breathe you however many Spells you want.'

'Many Sspellss?' Stubby Nose grinned wickedly. 'Do you promisse?'

'You helped my daughter.' Mam wrapped her arm about Rayne. 'I promise with all my heart.'

Rayne clambered into the boat and sat next to Tom. Mam pushed away from the quay.

'Did you know the Master and Frank were the same?' asked Rayne.

Mam shook her head. 'I've only known him as

Francis. I didn't know he'd become a shapeshifter. Somewhere along the way he must have crafted a Spell and persuaded someone to breathe it over him.'

Rayne stared into the dark water. 'I can't bear to think of him lying at the bottom.' She bit her lip. 'If only we'd breathed the breath-holding Spell over him, he might have had a chance.'

'Maybe we'll find him one day,' said Mam, but she didn't sound confident. 'Let's go home.'

'Home.' Tom let out a long sigh. 'It won't be though, will it?'

'Won't be what?'

'It won't be anything like home.'

NO PLACE LIKE HOME

Tom stowed the oars and the boat bumped against the riverbank.

Rayne scanned the trees. 'Are you sure this is the right place?'

'Look at the Penderin mountains,' he said, pointing to their snow-capped peaks. 'That's the view from my bedroom window. I'd know it anywhere.'

Mam clambered across the boat slats and grasped a tree branch. 'Good enough for me. Let's get out here.'

Catching a long tuft of grass, Rayne pulled herself up the bank. Tom and Mam followed and together they tied the boat's mooring rope around a tree trunk.

Mam wiped her palms on her skirt. 'See if you can find the white stone the warden uses to mark the bridge.'

'How will that help?' asked Tom. 'You don't have a Spell to let us across.'

'True, but they will see us and know we have returned. Then we can use the stone as a reference point to skirt the barrier and find your tunnel.'

A chill wind blew down from the mountains. Rayne hugged herself. 'How bad do you think it is in there?'

Mam shook her head sadly.

Rayne stared across the river. It was hard to believe that somewhere in the reflection of trees was their home. 'I wish Frank was here.'

Tom kicked at a clump of grass. 'Me too.'

She lifted a branch and walked underneath it. Her stomach churned, remembering the way Old Flo and the blacksmith had chased her across the village. When she got inside the barrier everyone would be angry. She couldn't blame them. She'd have to spend the rest of her life making up for it. But whatever she did, she knew it would never be enough.

A flash of white caught her eye. 'I think I've found it.' She jogged to the stone. 'It's here.' Bending to pull the grass clear she stopped suddenly. Propped against the stone was Mam's satchel. 'How?' She snatched it up. 'Mam! Come quickly!'

Mam rushed around the tree. 'What's the matter?'

Rayne swung around. *'Look.'*

Mam grasped the satchel. She tore it open and pulled out a red velvet book-shaped bundle. She peeled away the cloth and gasped. No longer smeared in mud, her cherry wood Spell book gleamed with polish. Quickly she turned its pages, a slow smile spreading across her face.

Hardly daring to believe it, Rayne peeped over Mam's shoulder. Joy blossomed. Every letter of every line was perfectly complete.

Mam shook her head. 'How did this get back to me?'

Rayne scanned the trees, hoping to see a snatch of red fur or a robe of golden quills.

'The Spell book is fixed?' Tom marched up to them. 'Everyone is . . . ?'

Mam's eyes sparkled. *'Everyone* in Penderin is well again.'

'How is this even possible?' he asked.

'I don't know, but I suspect we'll find out.' She brought out a sheaf of blank parchments from the satchel. Winking at Rayne, she laid the book on the grass and flipped the pages.

'Are you looking for the thinning Spell?'

'Something better. We don't need the barrier

any more.'

A golden waterfall of words cascaded from her head as she copied a Spell onto the sheet. Wrapping the book back in its cloth, she bundled it into the satchel and handed the Spell to Rayne. 'Will you?'

Smiling from ear to ear, Rayne turned to the water's edge and breathed over the Spell. The words streaked like lightning towards the river.

The air shimmered.

The barrier flashed like a mirror reflecting sunlight, then it vanished. In its place were rows of golden thatch and smoke curling from chimneys. The warden stood on the bridge, an arm raised in greeting, his smiling face no longer on his chest.

Mam laughed and wrapped her arms about Rayne and Tom. She guided them onto the bridge. 'Welcome home.'

Waiting on the other side were Tom's parents. He broke free and ran to meet them. Rayne watched as they wrapped their arms about him.

Owen and Jenna stood further back. Between them Little Jack bounced up and down.

Rayne drank it all in. 'Everyone is the same. No sign of plague.'

Mam tightened her arm. 'There'll be no plague anywhere in Penderin today.'

The warden greeted them. 'Good to see you, Meleri. And you, Rayne.' He rubbed his bristly chin. 'I am sorry for the other night. I rather lost my head.'

Rayne blushed. 'No, I'm sorry. Sorry for breaking the book. Sorry for making you sick.'

The warden sighed. 'What's done is done. We've been keeping together in the village hall. Those who could, looking after those who couldn't. But everything changed this morning when the plague left us, and we rejoiced, knowing our Spell Breathers had made all well.'

'It wasn't us,' said Mam. 'We came home expecting to help you as best we could.'

'It sounds like quite a story. Before you tell it, what's happened to the barrier? You've removed it completely.'

'It's all part of the story.' Mam grinned broadly. 'I'll skip to the ending. My sister pursues us no longer. We can leave the barrier open.'

The warden's eyes crinkled at the edges as he returned Mam's smile. 'I am glad.'

As they walked off the bridge Little Jack ran towards Mam and wrapped his arms around her legs. 'Welcome back, Spell Breather!'

Mam ruffled his hair. 'Thank you, little one. How are you?'

Jack held out his hands. 'All better now. Look, hands not paws.'

Jenna came up beside them. Rayne grasped her hands, relieved they were no longer twisted claws. 'I'm sorry. This was all my fault. It was never Tom's.'

'I know,' said Jenna. 'No one is angry now. You brought your mam home and made us well.'

Owen came up beside them. 'What's it like outside?'

'The barrier's staying down, so you can see for yourself,' said Rayne.

'Stranger on the bridge!' cried the warden, unsheathing his sword.

Rayne's head snapped around. A man stood on the far side. He had a crop of thick red hair, tied at the back of his neck. He looked straight at Rayne.

She whispered his name. 'Frank.'

The warden jogged onto the bridge, pointing his sword in front of him. 'Stay where you are!'

The man bowed. 'Please. I seek shelter.'

'You're not welcome here,' called the warden. 'For all we know, you may have the plague.'

'Do I look like a monster? If you let me cross, your Spell Breather can check me over.'

Mam walked alongside the warden and pushed her palm against the flat of his sword. 'Come into

Penderin. You are most welcome, friend.'

Rayne swallowed a lump in her throat.

Mam turned to the warden. 'This is who you must thank for healing the plague. His name is Frank and he's a Word Master.'

The warden sheathed his sword and offered his hand. 'You are very welcome, Word Master.'

They walked off the bridge towards Rayne. Her smile slipped a little as she saw Frank was limping. His face was a patchwork of cuts and bruises.

'Do not thank me,' said Frank. 'Rayne saved you all when she breathed a perfect word. Better than any Spell I have ever crafted.'

'I'm so glad you're safe,' said Rayne. 'We thought you'd drowned.'

'Drowned? My dear, you should know by now, I never drown.'

Tom ran up to them, a huge grin on his face. 'What happened to Staunch?'

'Swept away.' Frank's mouth twitched at the corners. 'I like to think the fish-brothers made him feel welcome.'

'But how did you get here so quickly? It's taken us days on the river.'

'After I repaired the Spell book . . .' His eyes slid to Mam. 'Mali sent me . . . by hand.'

'*What?*' said Mam. 'She used her power to control you again?'

Frank blushed. 'She begged me. I could not refuse. She is desperate to make amends, you know. Things are different. Even now, the Great Library is transforming. News of Mali's change of heart was spread by the birds. A handful of Spell Breathers who had kept themselves hidden for years have begun arriving.'

'Really?' said Rayne, her eyes shining. 'You mean me and Mam *aren't* the last Spell Breathers?'

'It seems not,' Frank answered them.

Mam folded her arms. 'As wonderful as that news is, the bump on your head is affecting your senses. You left my sister *alone* with other Spell Breathers?'

The sound of drums and pipes and of people shouting and laughing made them turn. Emerging from a row of cottages, the villagers of Penderin processed along the riverbank calling to their Spell Breather. Rayne spied the blacksmith, his ears back to normal size. And Old Flo leaning on her cane, her head firmly on her shoulders. The guilt she'd been carrying around for days completely fell away.

'Everyone wants to welcome you home,' said the warden, drawing Mam away. Little Jack skipped behind her. Jenna and Owen followed in his wake.

Frank held out his hands to Rayne and Tom. 'Do not leave. I have something to say.'

He dropped to his knees and hunched onto his elbows. Red fur sprouted across his cheeks and hands. His legs and arms rippled and shrunk, as they slid out of his clothes. Frank whipped his tail about his body.

Tom whistled. 'I'll never get used to that.'

'I am sorry for lying and leading you into danger.' Frank bowed his head. 'Your friendship and courage changed me in ways I could not imagine before we met. I am forever grateful.'

Rayne knelt. 'You helped us save Mam and you cured the plague. We are grateful to you.'

Frank raised amber eyes to her face. 'Will you do me the honour of calling me friend once more?'

Tom grinned. 'I wouldn't go that far.'

Frank's snout twitched. 'In the Scriptorium, you said you were beginning to like me.'

'Not fair.' Tom knelt beside Rayne. 'I didn't know I was talking to *you*.'

Rayne giggled. 'What will you do now? Will you stay with us?'

'For a short while. I am needed at the Great Library. There are many books to repair. And with Spell Breathers returning, there is even the possibility of apprentice school reopening.'

Tom leaned forward. 'Can I help you repair the books?'

'Huh?' Rayne nudged him in the shoulder. 'For years you've hated Spells and now you want to write them?'

Tom nudged her back. 'Someone's got to keep an eye on you Spell Breathers.'

'Do not take this the wrong way,' said Frank. 'Have you ever *read* a dictionary?

Tom rolled his eyes.

'And what about you, Rayne?' asked Frank. 'What will you do now?'

Rayne's eyes glowed. 'I am Mam's apprentice. I will train to be a Spell Breather.' She laughed. 'Mind you, after the excitement of the last few days, lessons may seem very dull.'

'Dull?' repeated Frank. He looked from Rayne to Tom and back again. 'I doubt that. Knowing you two, I doubt that very much.'

SPELL MAKING TOOL-KIT

Are you a budding Word Master? Would you like to write a Spell? Maybe, like Tom, you're keen to craft *The Spell of Flying*? Or maybe you can think of a special Spell of your own?

To write a Spell, all you need is big piece of paper, a pencil and a Thesaurus. If you don't have all those at home, you can easily find them at your local library.

Let's start by writing a flying Spell together. Then once you know how, you can have a go at writing your own Spell.

STEP #1

Write a list of words related to flying. There are lots of ways to fly; how many can you think of?

There are a few words on the next page to start you off:

Rise	Float
Swoop	Ascend
Drift	Soar

STEP #2

Once you have a list, look up each word in your Thesaurus to find more synonyms for flying. Add those to your list. Then look up some of the new words you just found to make your list bigger. The longer your list, the easier it will be to craft the exact Spell you want.

Here's how my list looks now . . .

Rise	Float
Swoop	Ascend
Descend	Drift
Sky	Soar
Glide	Flap
Waft	Race
Air	Clouds
Hover	Flutter
Flit	Whoosh
Sway	Hang

Zoom   Rush
Dash   Dart
Windborne   Scud
Levitate   Volitant

(This is a rare word. If you found it in your Thesarus the Word Masters would like to offer you an apprenticeship at the Great Library!)

STEP #3

Sift the words from your list into a rhyme. Here are a couple of ways the words from my list could form the start of different types of flying Spells. What sort of flying Spell do you think Tom would like? Do you think he wants to hover in the air or soar through the sky?

*S*pell of Flying
Rise, Flutter, Swoop
Spin, Soar, Loop

*S*pell of Flying
Hover, Waft, Glide
On fluffy clouds ride

STEP #4

Hmmm. I think Tom would love to soar. If you agree, then see what words you can take from your list to finish the Spell. As you write it, feel free to add words that aren't on the list, so you can make the Spell do precisely what you want. And remember to bring Tom back to the ground at the end, otherwise he'd be flying forever! Here's what I came up with . . .

Spell of Flying
Rise, Flutter, Swoop
Spin, Soar, Loop
Whoosh through the sky
Many miles high
Faster than sound
Descend home to the ground

I wonder how you will finish the Spell? Once it is complete, Tom might ask Rayne to breathe it over him, because of course word-magic won't work without a Spell Breather.

Now you know how to write a Spell, will you craft a special Spell of your own?

JULIE PIKE

JULIE PIKE is a graduate of the Bath Spa MA in Creative Writing for Young People. Julie is passionate about adventure stories and volunteers in local schools, helping children find stories that excite them. She loves real-life adventures too, and has travelled to the peak of Kilimanjaro, across the Tibetan Plains to Mount Everest, and skydived over New Zealand. When not reading, writing or adventuring, Julie works as a sustainability consultant—helping to care for the planet so future generations can enjoy their own adventures.

ACKNOWLEDGEMENTS

It takes a community to raise a book. I would be lost without mine. Eternal thanks to . . .

Wonderful editors Liz Cross and Gillian Sore, for sprinkling magic over the story and illuminating unexplored depths. Holly Fulbrook and Dinara Mirtalipova, for a cover that makes my heart sing. And the whole friendly team at OUP for your warm welcome.

Jo Williamson, my splendid agent, who perfectly combines sage advice with enthusiastic cheerleading.

The MA Writing for Young People at Bath Spa Uni. To our writing mum, Julia Green, for your wisdom and championing a course that changed my world. Lucy Christopher, for sharing that the best stories are filled with fear and excitement. And C J Skuse, for showing me the bomb under the bed.

MA friends for forensically cheering early instalments: Finbar Hawkins, Helen Lipscombe, Kirsty Applebaum, Maddy Woosnam, Christina Wheeler, Imogen Ridley, Anna Houghton, Beatrice Wallbank, Clare Furniss, and Elen Caldecott. Heartfelt gratitude to Zoe Cookson for being Tom's Fairy Godmother. And to Jacqui Catcheside, who knew all about Rayne before me; wherever you are, my lovely, I hope you agree I got there in the end.

Tremendous MA friends, Kathryn Clark and Sarah House, for twice critiquing full draft manuscripts and never tiring of the adventure.

The Society of Children's Book Writers and Illustrators, for your ocean of resources and support.

Gill Trueman, Librarian at Peasedown St John Primary School and her cohort of veracious readers, for your delight in the story and reigniting my excitement.

My brother David, for being my fellow adventurer and not minding about slipping down the face of a snowy mountain. Mam, for tenderly breathing the Spell of Stories over us. And Dad, for showing me the magic in a dictionary.

My husband Rob Griffiths, for filling my writing cave with love, time, good coffee, and always believing.

Cathryn Hindle, for dreaming with me beside an open window and being there when the first words were written down. And Hamish and Luke Everett, for kindly liking my first attempt at a chapter.

Last, but never least, Steve Voake, for your wonderful writing prompt at Arvon. Who'd have thought that lost girl with a fox fur draped across her shoulders would lead to this? Thanks for the idea spark and aeons of patient guidance. Dear reader, if you want to write, find yourself on a Steve Voake workshop. Truly, it's where the magic begins.

Ready for more great stories? Try one of these ...

JULIA GREEN

To the Edge of the World

MIDNIGHT AT MOONSTONE

A MAGICAL MUSEUM WITH A LIFE OF ITS OWN

WRITTEN BY LARA FLECKER

ILLUSTRATED BY TRISHA KRAUSS

CERRIE BURNELL

The GIRL with the SHARK'S TEETH

THE Closest Thing to Flying

GILL LEWIS